A threat to the ranch

Damaged, Obsolete, Surplus
Jackson County Library Services
WITHDRAWN

"What did Elsa say?"

"Huh? Well, she said 'cluck' about fifty times."

"Is that all?"

"No sir, I finally got it out of her and . . ." He glanced over his shoulder and moved closer. "Pooch, this is liable to throw a scare into you. I want you to be ready for it."

"I'm ready, so hurry up."

"Well sir, what she heard was a whole army of coyotes out there in the wilderness—screeching and hollering and carrying on like I don't know what."

The word *coyotes* sent a shiver through my body. I moved closer. "Yes? Carrying on about what? Details, J.T., I need details."

He leaned closer. "Elsa said they were singing about . . . chickens."

D0171390

The Case of
the Coyote Invasion

John R. Erickson

Illustrations by Gerald L. Holmes

Maverick Books, Inc.

MAVERICK BOOKS, INC.

Published by Maverick Books, Inc.

P.O. Box 549, Perryton, TX 79070

Phone: 806.435.7611

www.hankthecowdog.com

First published in the United States of America by Viking Children's Books and
Puffin Books, members of Penguin Putnam Books for Young Readers, 2010.
Currently published by Maverick Books, Inc., 2013

1   3   5   7   9   10   8   6   4   2

Copyright © John R. Erickson, 2010

All rights reserved

CIP DATA IS AVAILABLE UPON REQUEST

Maverick Books, Inc. ISBN 978-1-59188-156-8

Hank the Cowdog® is a registered trademark of John R. Erickson.

Printed in the United States of America

Except in the United States of America, this book is sold subject to the condition that
it shall not, by way of trade or otherwise, be lent, re-sold, hired out, or otherwise
circulated without the publisher's prior consent in any form of binding or cover
other than that in which it is published and without a similar condition
including this condition being imposed on the subsequent purchaser.

For my friends,
Nancy, Rick, and Michael Pearcey

CONTENTS

Cheapo Brand Dog Food

It's me again, Hank the Cowdog. Through our network of spies and undercover agents, we learned that the coyotes were planning a big raid on the chicken house, but that came after the Birdseed Fiasco. I would rather not discuss the BSF, but I guess we must, since it helps explain a few details about the coyote invasion.

See, it wasn't my fault. If the people around here didn't want me stealing birdseed, they should have put some decent food in my dog bowl. What's a dog to do when they put out slop for the dogs? I don't expect steak for every meal, but for crying out loud!

Okay, let's slow down and take this one step at a time. I can point to the very moment this whole

1

mess began, Friday afternoon at five o'clock. On a lot of outfits, five o'clock on Friday afternoon means quitting time, the start of a long weekend of fun, frolic, and goofing off. On this ranch, it means nothing of the kind. It means that another endless day of work is fixing to melt into an endless night of work, then another day and another night, on and on.

We have no weekends around here, just work and more work. Am I complaining? No sir. Work is what I do. It's what I *want* to do. All I expect is a place to sleep and enough Co-op dog food to keep me going. But, see, that's where the whole problem began.

At five o'clock that Friday afternoon, Loper returned from a trip to town, wheeled into headquarters, and stopped his pickup in front of the machine shed. I happened to be there and saw the whole thing. He stepped out of the pickup and gave me a grin.

"Hank, this is a good day. I've figured out how to cut ten bucks a month off my dog food bill."

Somehow, that didn't thrill me, so I went to Slow Puzzled Wags on the tail section.

He continued. "There's a new store in town: The House of Thrift. Their motto is, 'We'd skin a flea and sell the hide.'" He chuckled and gave me a wink. "It's a cowboy kind of store, and they've got their own line of dog food." He pointed to a fifty-pound sack in the back of the pickup. "Cheapo Brand dog food. You're going to love this, pooch."

Oh really?

Chuckling to himself, he opened a corner of the sack and filled the overturned Ford hubcap that served as our dog bowl. "Okay, bud, dig in. Tell me what you think."

I moved my nose closer to the heap of brownish kernels and gave it a sniffing. We've discussed Co-op brand dog food, right? It has the smell of stale grease. This stuff had the smell of . . . I couldn't even describe it. Bad.

I gave him Sad Eyes and Slow Wags, as if to say, "You're kidding, right? This is a joke?"

His smile faded. "Hank, this isn't the Waldorf-Astoria. Give it a try, you might be surprised."

Okay, I gave it a try, one bite, and sure enough, I was surprised. It tasted even worse than I'd expected. It was like cardboard. Goat droppings. I backed away from the bowl and used my tongue to sweep the crumbs out of my mouth.

Angry lines gouged a path across Loper's face. "Well, it's dog food, and you're a dog. When you get hungry, you'll eat it." He went to the house,

shaking his head and muttering about "fussy eaters."

Oh yeah? When I got hungry, I might eat tree bark, but I would NOT eat Cheapo. What an outrage, feeding such garbage to the Head of Ranch Security! For years I had put up with the Co-op brand and that had been bad enough, but this stuff made Co-op look like a gourmet meal.

If he thought Cheapo was so good, he ought to eat it himself . . . but of course that would never happen. The people around here would never think of eating anything that came out of a fifty-pound sack, but when it comes to their dogs . . . oh well.

You'll be proud to know that I imposed a boycott on all Cheapo products. Friday night, I went to bed hungry and by Saturday morning, I was weak from poor nutrition. We're talking about trembling, stomach growling, hardly able to walk, the whole nine yards of food deprivation.

And that's what led to the problem with the birdseed. See, I never would have considered . . . we'll get to that in a minute.

For now, let's set the stage. Saturday morning came right after Friday night, and Sally May had made plans to drive into town and spend the afternoon, doing . . . what was it? Scrapbooking.

She was going to attend a class on how to make scrapbooks, and she had lined up Loper to babysit the children.

And, naturally, I would be in charge of the rest of the ranch while she was gone. No problem there, except that I was in the middle of a Food Boycott.

When Sally May and Little Alfred came out of the house that morning, everybody seemed to be in a good mood. That was important. See, I want My People to be happy and, you know, satisfied that the world is treating them right. I can't always solve their problems, but by George, I always try—especially when it comes to Sally May, our Beloved Ranch Wife. I lie awake at night, trying to think of ways to make myself the Dog of Her Dreams.

Anyway, I noticed that she and Alfred were out in the backyard, doing something, so I went down to check it out. Since dogs weren't allowed inside her yard, I stayed outside the fence. Pete, her precious kitty, could come and go as he wished, but the Head of Ranch Security was banned.

That was really weird, but never mind. Since I wasn't allowed inside the yard, I had to do my observing from outside, and here's what I saw. Alfred and Sally May pounded a metal post into the ground, just below the kitchen window. On top of the post was a piece of flat metal, a kind of platform, and on that platform they placed a little wooden house. It was about two feet long and one foot wide, and had the kind of slanted roof that you find on ordinary houses where people live.

You're probably wondering why they had put a little house on top of a metal stake. I wondered about that, too. I mean, it looked like a house but a house for *what*? I activated Visual Scanners and took a closer look.

Hmmm. This was interesting. Sally May removed the roof of the little house and poured something inside, and you'll never guess what it was. Give up?

Birdseed.

Yes sir, birdseed, and that gave me the clue I needed to crack this mystery. See, it looked like a house, but it was actually a *bird feeder* in the shape of a house, and that's why she poured birdseed inside. Just follow the logic on this: seed-feed-feeder.

At that moment, Drover, my assistant, joined me. "Gosh, what a cute little house. Who's going to live in it?"

"Nobody's going to live in it, because it's not a house. It's a bird feeder."

"They're feeding the birds?"

"Correct, and don't ask me why."

7

He gave it a closer look. "How come they're feeding birds?"

"I just told you not to ask."

"Sorry. You don't know?"

"I have no idea. Why would anyone put out feed for birds? If you feed them, they'll hang around."

He sat down and scratched a spot on his ribs. "Well, maybe Sally May likes to watch the birds while she's working in the kitchen."

"Maybe so, but it seems a foolish waste of time. Why would she want to watch a bunch of sniveling birds when she could watch ... well, us for example?"

He gave me a silly grin. "Well, we don't do much."

"*You* don't do much. For your information, I put in eighteen hours a day on this ranch, but do these people ever take the time to watch me? Do they notice all the things I do to keep this outfit running? Oh no, they want to watch birds."

"Well, birds are kind of pretty. Oh look." He pointed toward the yard. Sally May and Alfred had gone back into the house, and a bird had come to the feeder. "It's a cardinal."

I squinted toward the feeder. "That bird isn't a cardinal, he's a moocher. He's stealing birdseed."

"Well, I think the whole idea is for the birds to eat the seeds."

I glared down at the runt. "Drover, the bird is a moocher. Furthermore, he makes noise, and I don't like birds. If you want to sit here and watch moocher-birds all day, that's fine, but I have a ranch to run."

I whirled away and left him sitting in the shubbles of his own rubble. The very idea! I mean, who has time to sit around and watch a bunch of little tweet-tweets stealing birdseed? Not me.

But you know what? I found myself watching them anyway and, just as I expected, what I saw really got under my skin—a constant parade of cardinals, twitteries, tweeties, sparrows, and other birds with two wings and a beak. Dozens of birds. I didn't want to get involved in a bird situation, but those bums were stealing us blind and someone needed to do something.

So I did what any normal American dog would have done. I went back to the yard fence, set up a firing position near the gate, and made preparations to bark at the birds. For some reason, Drover began backing away, then vanished like a puff of smoke. That was fine. I didn't want him distracting me when I began lobbing Mortar Barks at the feeder.

My barrage of barking worked like a charm. After five minutes of steady barking, I had cut the crime rate by 63 percent. Another thirty minutes, and I would have . . .

The back door opened, and out stepped Sally May. Good. She had seen my work, and I knew that she would be . . .

"Hank, stop barking at the birds!"

Huh?

"You're scaring them away."

Well, sure, but that was the whole point. See . . .

"Find something else to do, and leave my birds alone." *Slam!* She went back into the house.

Well, what do you say? I couldn't think of anything. It left me speechless. She didn't seem to understand what was going on in her own yard. I was about to leave the promises . . . the premises, let us say . . . I was about to leave the premises of the promises when something else caught my eye.

It had four legs, hair, and a tail. It was rubbing its way down the fence, and it wore an annoying smirk on its mouth. You'll never guess what it was.

A cat.

I Steal a Great Idea
from the Cat

I wasn't in the mood for Pete. I'm very seldom in the mood for Pete, but here he came. I braced myself for his usual greeting: "My, my, it's Hankie the Wonderdog!"

But that's not what he said. In a fairly civil tone of voice, he said, "Well, good morning, Hank."

For the second time in a span of mere minutes, I found myself speechless. But also suspicious. Why would Pete, a professional smart aleck, call me by my proper name and wish me good morning? It didn't add up. I mean, we've discussed my Position on Cats, right? I don't like 'em, never have, and I had plenty of reason to think that Pete didn't like me either.

What was going on here?

I studied him with a wary eye as he came sliding down the fence. He stopped, sat down, curled his tail around his body, and said, "I saw what happened."

"Oh? Well, I'm sure you enjoyed watching me get scolded by the lady of the house. That's okay, laugh it up, I don't care."

"Actually . . . no. I thought it was unfair."

That word caused me to flinch. "You thought it was unfair? Ha ha. Sorry, Kitty, but I find that hard to believe."

"It's true. I sensed that you were trying to help."

"Of course I was trying to help. For the past hour, those birds have been stealing grain."

He turned his gaze toward the sky. "I know, Hankie, and you were probably concerned about how much it's costing the ranch."

"You bet I was. I mean, to save money, Loper just switched me over to Cheapo dog food, yet those birds are gobbling down expensive birdseed like there's no tomorrow. Within a week, this ranch could be in trouble. It all comes down to management, Pete. If you don't control expenses, you're going broke."

He gave his head a sad shake. "See? I understand that. It's simple accounting, isn't it?"

"Right. You've got your debbles and your

crebbles. If the two columns don't match, you're going broke and don't know it. Mark my words, Pete, those birds are going to get this ranch into serious financial problems."

"I couldn't agree more, Hankie." He studied his paw for a moment. "I don't understand why Sally May pampers them so."

"Great word, Pete, I like that. 'Pampers.' That's exactly what she does."

His eyes drifted around and landed on me. "That feed she's giving them . . . it must be the very best money can buy. The birds just love it."

I paced a few steps away. "Pete, you've hit the nail right on the donkey. They buy high-dollar feed for a bunch of worthless never-sweat tweetie birds, but what do they put out for the Head of Ranch Security? Cheapo Brand dog slop . . . in an old Ford hubcap!"

"This is so sad."

"It's worse than sad. It's disgraceful, outrageous. But when I tried to help, Sally May screeched at me. Pete, sometimes I think this is a lousy job."

The cat rolled over on his back and began slapping at his tail. "I wonder what Cheapo Brand dog food is made of?"

"Goat droppings, potato peelings, and garbage. Why do you ask?"

"Oh, nothing. I'm sure you wouldn't be interested."

I marched back to him. "I probably won't, but let's hear it. I mean, you're just a dumb little ranch cat, but every once in a while you come up with an idea."

"Oh, thank you, Hankie. I'm not used to getting compliments from you."

"Yeah, well, don't get used to it, because it might not happen again." I glanced over both shoulders to make sure Drover wasn't spying on us, then leaned toward the cat. "Talk to me, Pete. What kind of scheme are you cooking up?"

"No scheme, Hankie, just a thought. If birdseed is better than dog food, maybe the birds should be eating the dog food." He delivered a hard slap to his tail. "And maybe you should be eating . . . birdseed."

I stared into his yellowish eyes. "You're joking, right? Dogs don't eat birdseed."

"Why not?"

"Because . . . I don't know, because we don't. It seems unnatural, a dog eating bird food."

"Eating garbage seems natural?"

"I didn't say that. My only point is . . ." I paced a few steps away. I mean, my mind was really spinning. "It's an interesting idea, Pete, and over the next few days, I'll give it some thought. We probably won't use it, but if we do . . . hey, I'll see that you get a little reward."

"Oh, thank you, Hankie. Maybe you could even share some of the birdseed with me." He grinned and fluttered his eyelids.

I paced back to him. "I said it was an interesting idea, but don't let it go to your head. Good ideas are a dime a dozen around here, and most of them never make it past the Executive Committee. We'll take it up at our next meeting, that's all I can promise. Well, it was nice talking to you."

"Is someone leaving?"

"Correct. You. I don't mean to be rude, Pete, but . . ." I glanced over my shoulders. "Look, pal, it wouldn't do my reputation any good if someone saw us talking."

"Ohhhh, good point!" He leaped to his feet and gave me a wink. "I'll run along, and nobody will ever know."

"Thanks, Pete, I appreciate your attitude. I mean, you and I don't make the rules, but we do have to live with them."

"You're right, Hankie, tee hee."

"What?"

He began walking away. "I said, you're right. The world isn't a perfect place."

"Exactly. One of these days, maybe cats and dogs can dare to be friends, but . . . well, we're not there yet. See you around."

He waved one last good-bye and vanished around the north side of the house. At that point, I indulged myself in a rush of inward laughter and celebration. Do you see what this meant? Ho! I had just conned the cat out of a great idea!

Maybe you missed it, so let me explain. Using clever interrogation techniques, I had coaxed some extremely important information out of the kitty. Here, take a look at my notes of the interrogation.

TOP SECRET
file#C3PO Pete Interrogation

Birdseed is expensive.

Cheapo Brand dog food is cheap.

Expensive is always better than cheap, therefore bird food is better than dog food.

Dogs deserve the best food money can buy.

Birds, who contribute nothing to the ranch, deserve the worst food money can buy.

Dogs are bigger than birds and can beat them up, in case the birds want to argue about it. Heh heh.

End of File. Please Destroy at Once!

Pretty awesome, huh? You bet. By merely switching food supplies, we could introduce balance and justice into the universe, while investing ranch dollars in our most important asset—ME.

Wow! You talk about a great concept! This was a work of art, so beautiful that it almost brought tears to my eyes.

And the best part about it, the very very best part, was that I had STOLEN the idea from Pete! Ha ha! I had promised to give him a "little reward," remember? Well, I would deliver on that promise . . . and give him the *littlest* reward that money could buy: absolutely nothing.

Ha ha, hee hee, ho ho. I loved it!

Well, why not? Pete had built his whole career on luring me into traps and getting me into trouble, so this was just payback, and long overdue. After years of taking his trash, I had finally caught him in a careless moment. I was fixing to put his scheming little mind to work for the side of Truth and Justice.

This was great. In one big game on the Chessboard of Life, I had solved the Bird Problem, the Dog Food Problem, and the Kitty Problem, all in one grand swoop.

Hee hee. Sorry, I shouldn't gloat . . . but you know what? I'm going to gloat anyway. Watch this:

Gloat gloat!

Hey, this is fun.

Gloat gloat!

Hee hee. Whoever said that gloating isn't good wholesome entertainment has never tried it. Take it from a guy who knows, gloating is good for the body and good for the soul. It's inexpensive, low in carbo-whatnots, and high in villimuns, and it beats all the alternatives by a mile.

Boy, what a triumph, but it was time to stop celebrating and get to work. I turned my enormous body around and faced the yard. The bird feeder was waiting.

CHAPTER THREE

We Launch the Mission

The bird feeder was waiting, and the Parade of Birds had moved into high gear. I mean, I had never dreamed that we had so many deadbeat moocher-birds on the ranch. Dozens of them. Hundreds of them, even!

But before I could put my plan into action, I had to make sure that You Know Who wasn't looking out the kitchen window with her radar eyes. Maybe you'd forgotten about the Sally May Factor, but I hadn't. This was the one part of the plan over which I had no control. If she was hovering around the window, we would have to cancel the mission.

See, long-term experience with Sally May had made me cautious. Just when you think she's not around, she'll come flying out the door and nail you with that broom. A guy can't afford to be careless. But our intelligence reports gave us reason to hope. Remember that she was planning on going to town? If she was going to town, she would have to get ready, and if she had to get ready, she wouldn't be lurking around the kitchen window.

Pretty shrewd, huh? You bet.

Before sending troops over the wall, we did a procedure called "casing the joint." It's a special technique we use in our work and it means— walking around the area, looking very casual, whistling a little tune, and pretending to be doing . . . well, nothing, just taking a stroll and enjoying the morning air.

When it's done right, any witnesses on the scenery will think, "Well, there's a normal dog doing normal things." No witness would ever think, "That dog is fixing to jump into the yard and burglarize the bird feeder."

After casing the joint for five minutes, I came up with the answer I had been looking for. Sally May had left the kitchen, and we had a GO for the mission. The only witnesses to the crime . . . to the, uh, mission would be a bunch of brainless tweetie birds, and who pays attention to them? Nobody.

The time had come. I squared my enormous

shoulders and filled my tanks with a fresh supply of carbon diego. Where I was going, I would need it. I turned toward the east, paced up to the yard fence, went into Deep Crouch, and launched myself over the top.

Inside the yard, I paused to reconoodle the situation and switched on the microphone of my mind. "Control, this is Righteous. We have boots on the ground. Repeat: we have boots on the ground and no sign of Sally May. Request permission to proceed with the mission, over."

The radio crackled, and I heard the voice of Control. "Uh, roger, Righteous, we copy. You have permission to proceed. Good hunting."

"Roger that, Control. We're going in."

I crept forward until I came to the post on which the feeder was perched. I rolled my gaze upward and saw five red birds looking down at me with puzzled expressions. I lifted my lips into a snarl and growled, "Take a hike, you slackers!"

One nice thing about birds is that they're all chickens. Let me rephrase that. The birds I saw weren't actually chickens. They were cardinals, but at a deeper level, they were chickenhearted. That was important information, for it meant that when push came to shovel, they would run from a fight.

And they did. When they saw my fangs gleaming in the morning sun, they wanted none of me and flew away. Okay, they didn't actually run from a fight (they flew), but the result was the same. We were able to secure the bird feeder without casualties, bloodshed, or the kind of barking, squawking, and flapping that might arouse suspicion inside the house.

At that point, I activated Pumps One and Two and went into Hydraulic Lift on the hind legs. Making no more noise than a mouse, I rose into the air until I was able to rest my front paws on the metal platform. There, I switched off pumps and began probing the feeder with Noseatory Sensors.

Sniff, sniff.

Lines of data flashed across the console of my mind: "Millet, barley, oats, and several unidentified types of grain. High-quality bird food, worth capturing."

Well, that's what we needed to know. I leaned closer and activated our Robot Tongue mechanism, unrolling three inches of tongue, just enough to do the job without getting ourselves overextended. The tongue mechanism moved out, entered the pile of grain, and formed a curl on the end.

This was a pretty delicate procedure. Imagine

a dog operating a robot arm from inside the cabin of a spaceship. You're sitting there, surrounded by switches and blinking lights, and you have a control lever in each hand. Through the window, you can see the robot arm out there in space, and everything is done with instruments.

Same deal here, very delicate procedure. See, once you've put a curl in the end of the tongue, you have to reverse the hydraulics and bring the tongue back home, dragging a little pile of Product. (In these operations, we don't describe the material we're retrieving. We just call it Product. Why? Because . . . I'm not sure. I guess it sounds more official when you call it "Product" instead of "birdseed.")

Where were we? Oh yes, very delicate procedure, retrieving Product. Slowly, inch by inch, we maneuvered the Robot Tongue back to the ship and swept the first load into the Receiving Bay (mouth). There, we went to Jaws and Teeth and began processing the seeds.

Hmmm. They tasted exactly like . . . well, birdseed, but not bad. Pretty good, in fact, better than the petrified pellets that came out of a sack of Cheapo dog food. Okay, we would go back for another load.

Out went the Robot Tongue . . . activate curl . . .

drawback . . . docking . . . capture . . . process Product . . . over and over. It was slow, tedious, brackbucking work, but well worth the effort. Hey, I'd had no idea that birdseed was so good. Why had we been wasting it on the birds?

As I recall, we were deep into the mission and had processed, oh, fifteen loads of Product when a problem arose: two shrieking blue jays began dive-bombing the Command Module. Have we discussed blue jays? Maybe not. They are the most obnoxious birds on the ranch. Unlike the cardinals and sparrows and other birds, they will fight over food, and when they swoop down and peck you on the head, you know you've been pecked.

We took two hits right away. I went to the Emergency Frequency. "Control, we have a problem, enemy blue jays. They came out of nowhere . . . ouch . . . and they're not kidding, over."

The voice on the radio said, "Sic 'em, boy! Git 'em!"

Okay, we'd gotten clearance to fire back and we rigged for combat—Laser-Guided Tooth Cannons, VHF radar, the whole nine yards. Those birds were fixing to pay a price for their foolish behavior.

They swooped up into the air, made a circle, and came back for another bombing run. We had 'em on radar all the way. "Bearing two-five-zero!

Range fifteen yards and closing fast! Flood tubes one and three and fire electrically!"

Here they came! We launched our missiles and . . . well, missed. Somehow the pesky things slipped though and . . . RAT-TAT-TAT-TAT . . . landed a lucky shot . . . or two . . . okay, five or six, right on top of my head.

Okay, that did it! This was war! Hank the Cowdog does not take trash off a blue jay. Our missiles and torpedoes had failed, so it was time to go to old-fashioned hand-to-hand combat— swords, knives, clubs, you name it. I swiveled myself around . . .

CRASH!

Huh?

Did you hear that? Maybe not, because you weren't there, but I heard it, a loud crashing sound, almost as though . . . oops. You know, that bird feeder wasn't bolted down to the platform and somehow, in all the smoke and confusion of combat, I must have . . . uh . . . nudged it off the stand, so to speak.

And there it lay on the ground, beside a scatter of birdseed.

Oops.

Then another sound broke the eerie silence— the sound of a door opening. Gulp. I wasn't sure I wanted to see this, but, well, we needed to know what sort of crisis we were facing. Slowly, I turned my eyes toward the house and . . .

Oh no, it was HER!

There she stood on the porch, half her hair up in curlers and the other half . . . well, looking a lot like a buzzard's nest. She wore a robe and slippers, and maybe she had just stepped out of the shower. In her right hand, she carried . . . was that a gun? No, only a hairbrush. Whew!

A wide range of emotions flashed across her face: astonishment, anger, rage, fury . . . but then . . . holy smokes, she started laughing. "Alfred, come quick and bring the camera! You've got to see this! *Your father's dog is eating birdseed!*"

You know, sometimes a guy doesn't know what to do. Run? Hide? Pose for the camera? It was very confusing, but as I always say, when Sally May's laughing and not swinging her broom, things could be worse.

Okay, she wanted a picture, so I ignored all my instincts to run and waited for the camera to arrive.

It was very stressful, being there alone with Sally May. After several moments of laughing, she got control of herself and said, "Hank, what on earth are you doing?"

Well, that was . . . that was hard to explain. See,

her husband had dumped garbage into my dog bowl, and I'd been watching those birds and they were gobbling all of her feed and . . . oh brother, there was no way I could explain it. This was one of those moments when a dog has to hope that his people will, uh, try to understand.

Little Alfred came flying out the door. When he saw me, he burst out laughing. "He was eating out of the bird feeder?"

Oh brother.

Sally May held up the camera and snapped a picture, so now they had a photographic record of Hank the Cowdog in one of his most awkward moments. Great.

Well, the camera session was over, and what was I supposed to do now? Sally May stood on the porch for a long moment, biting back her smile, rolling her eyes, and shaking her head. Then she looked me straight in the eyes and said . . . this is a direct quote . . . she said, "Hank, you are SO DUMB!"

Yes ma'am.

"Now, get out of my yard and don't come back! Hike, scat!"

Yes ma'am.

I swept up the pieces of my shattered dignity, held my head at a proud angle, and marched away from this shameful episode. It almost broke my heart when I heard Little Alfred say, "I can't wait to tell Dad!"

Great. Everybody on the ranch would know about it, and I would be hearing about it until the end of time.

Healing Waters

You know, when a dog has passed through a stressful situation, he needs time to recover ... heal his spirit ... rebuild his broken self-esteemer.

A lot of dogs would have slunk away and gone into hiding for days. That's what Drover would have done. Not me. See, I was lucky enough to have my own Recovery Center, a place I could go to restore my spirit and bodily fluids.

We called it Emerald Pond because of its emerald green waters, fed by mineral springs that bubbled from deep under the septic tank. Many a time I had entered those healing waters as a broken dog, and had emerged an hour later, refreshed, restored, and ready to carry on my life's work.

And there was an added bonus. The same

waters that healed a broken spirit also had a powerful effect on the ladies. Those lady dogs just flipped over that deep manly aroma, which was no bad deal. I mean, with the womenfolk, a guy needs all the help he can get.

I left the yard and ran as fast as I could to Emerald Pond. I paused for a moment on the eastern shore, filled my nostrils with the aroma of herbs and spices, and plunged into the water's warm embrace. Oh yes! I could feel the tonic rushing through my . . .

Burp.

Birdseed. You know, it had tasted good, even delicious, but sometimes a guy gets carried away. I mean, just because one or two bites are good, that doesn't mean he ought to eat twenty-five pounds of the stuff. Moderation. That's the rule we should live by, moderation in all . . .

Bork.

. . . things, and it was becoming clear that I had sailed right past moderation and had made of a pig of myself. That happens in the best of families and it's no cause for . . . burp . . . shame, but something had to be done about the stupid birdseed.

I waded back to the shore and went straight into a Poison Alert, rocked my head back and forth five times, bent my head to the ground, and pulled

the Flush lever. In seconds, the whole unpleasant incident was behind me . . . in front of me, actually, on the ground. I found myself staring at this glop of toxic material and wondering . . .

You know, there are times when a dog searches his mind for answers and, well, he just doesn't find any. Birdseed? WHY?

I was lost in these dreary thoughts when something caught my eye. I lifted my head and saw . . . Drover. He was sitting about five feet away, gawking at me and wearing a silly grin.

"Oh, hi."

"Must you stare at me?"

"Well, I was just . . ."

I rumbled over to him. "Drover, did you come here to mock and ridicule?"

"No, I just wondered . . ."

"If you must know, that is what birdseed looks like after it has entered a dog's stomach and poisoned his system."

He started laughing. "Hee hee. It's a joke, right? Dogs don't eat birdseed."

"I ate birdseed! There's the proof on the ground, and I'd be grateful if you would wipe that insolent smirk off your mouth."

"Sorry. Hee hee."

"I heard that!"

He wiped the smirk off his mouth. "Sorry, but I never heard of a dog eating bird food. You really did?"

"Yes!"

He blinked his eyes, and there was a moment of silence. "How come?"

"Drover, everyone on the ranch is asking that question. I am asking that question." I stomped a few steps away and stared off into the distance. "All I can say is that, at the time, it struck me as a great idea."

"I'll be derned. Was it?"

"What do you think?"

"Well . . . I'd say maybe not."

"Drover, have you ever done anything . . . really ridiculous?"

"Well, let me think. No, I don't think so."

I whirled around and gave him a scorching glare. "Don't give me that! You've spent half your life being ridiculous. You were born ridiculous."

"That's what I meant."

"Then try to show some compassion for those of us who . . ." Suddenly I felt overwhelmed and sank to the ground. "I can't believe I did it! Drover, what kind of dog would put his reputation on the line . . . *to rob a bird feeder?*"

Drover drifted over and sat down beside me. "You really did that, no fooling?"

"Yes, yes, and yes! It was the dumbest stunt I've ever pulled."

"Huh. You weren't talking to Pete, were you?"

I raised my head and stared into the vacuum of his eyes. "Why would you ask a question like that?"

"Oh, I don't know. Sometimes when things go to blazes, you find cat tracks."

"Cat tracks? What are you saying, Drover, that I might have been dumb enough to be manipulated by the cat? Is that what you're saying?"

"I wondered."

"Well, you can stop wondering because there is absolutely no . . ." I cut my eyes from side to side. "Wait a second. I *was* talking to the little creep." I leaped to my feet. "And we were discussing birdseed. Don't you get it? This explains everything. I got sandbagged by the cat!"

"Boy, what a relief."

"Relief! Where's the relief?"

"Well . . . you're not as crazy as we thought . . . I guess."

"Dunce! I was crazy enough to get sandbagged by a cat and crazy enough to eat fifty pounds of birdseed! How crazy do you want me to be?"

"Well . . . let me think about that."

"They have pictures, Drover, it's all on film. There's no way I can say it didn't happen. And the sneaking, slimy, sniveling, slithering little crook of a cat lured me right into it!"

"Hee hee hee!"

"What?"

"I said . . . ouch. I'll bet that hurts."

I collapsed on the ground and let out a moan. "I'm ruined. Ruined!"

He gave me a pat on the shoulder. "Well, you can always look at the bright side."

Drover's words cheered me enough so that I was able to sit up. "Yes? Tell me about the bright side."

"Well . . . I haven't found it yet, but I'm thinking."

"There's no bright side, Drover. This time, the cat has really cooked my wagon."

"I rode in a wagon once."

"I'll never hear the end of this."

"Wagons are fun."

"They'll still be laughing when the snow flies."

"Yeah, they've been pretty bad."

"What?"

"The flies. They're really bad this year." Suddenly he snapped a fly out of the air. "See? I got one!"

"You ate a fly? Drover, that's disgusting."

"Well, you ate birdseed."

"Yes, and that's my whole point. You're eating flies, I ate birdseed . . . Drover, something has gone terribly wrong with the Security Division! We're all behaving like lunatics!"

Silence moved over us like a deadly cloud. Then . . . Drover's teeth clicked. "Got another one!"

"Drover, will you please try to be serious? Our department has sunk to the lowest level in . . . wait! I just thought of the brighter side. I'll apologize to Sally May!" I began pacing, as I often do when my mind has shifted to a higher level. "She's a good woman, kind and gentle . . . although she doesn't seem terribly fond of dogs."

"Oh, I think it's just you."

"If I make a full confession and throw myself at her mercy, maybe she can find it in her heart to forgive and forget."

"Yeah, I forget things all the time." He snapped at a fly. "Hey, I got another one!"

"Drover, please show some respect. I'm exposing my soul to you and . . . spit out that fly!"

He turned away from me. "It's mine."

"Spit it out this very minute, and that is a direct order!"

"Darn." He spat it out.

"Thank you. How can I reveal my deepest thoughts when you're . . ." All at once, a fly drilled me on the left ear, and we're talking about serious drilling. It hurt like crazy. I shucked him off the ear and then blasted him out of the air. "There, you little heathen, take that!"

"Did you get him?"

"You bet I got him. Ha. That fly has fled to the place where fallen flies flee."

"His name was Fred?"

"What?"

Drover scowled. "I thought you said the fly was Fred . . . and he bled red . . . or something like that."

"I did not say anything of the kind. There was no fly named Fred. Flies don't have names."

"I wonder why."

"I don't know why, I don't care. What was I talking about?"

"Some guy named Fred."

"Yes, of course." I resumed my pacing. "There was this dog named Fred, see, and I met him at a ranch rodeo. He was sitting in the back of a big Dodge pickup with a Cummins diesel engine, and he thought he was hot stuff. He started running his big mouth . . ." I heard a door slam down at the house. I stopped in my tracks and turned to Drover. "It's Sally May."

"You said it was Fred."

"She's leaving for town!"

"I thought it was a rodeo. Boy, I get confused."

"Drover, this is my opportunity to set things straight with the Lady of the House. I must go to her!"

I turned and made a dash for the house. Behind me, I heard a faint voice. "Wait, you just got out of the sewer!"

It was Drover's voice, but I didn't have time to think about what he'd said. And that was fine. Listening to Drover can rot your mind.

Spurned by
Sally May

As I went streaking toward the house, I had only one thought shining in the part of my mind that hadn't been rotted away by Drover's nonsense: *I had to set things straight with Sally May.*

Yes, it was time for us to heal all the wounds that had kept us apart for so many years. It was time for me to confess and time for her to forgive. This tension between us had gone on long enough.

I only hoped that I could get there in time, before she sped away and drove all the way into town with this burden on her heart. Brooding is bad for people, for dogs, for all creatures on this earth. It's much better to get everything out into

the open—to share, to cry, to laugh. It cleanses the soul.

A lot of dogs wouldn't have gone to all this trouble. When things go sour at the house, they just shrug and say, "So what?" Not me, fellers. Beneath all the iron and steel, I have a tender heart, and it won't rest until things are right.

As I went ripping past the machine shed, I saw her coming out of the house, and my heart leaped for joy. She hadn't left yet! She was wearing a pretty white dress. She'd fixed her hair, and I noticed a kind of glow on her face. She looked beautiful and happy and excited about having an afternoon to herself.

Yes, this was the time to work things out.

Loper came out on the porch, holding Baby Molly in his arms and waving good-bye. "Have a great time, hon."

Little Alfred was there, too, and he waved goodbye. "Bye, Mom! We'll miss you."

She came out the gate, glowing like the morning sun. She walked toward the car. I would have to pick up the pace to get there before she drove away. See, I already had this deal planned out. It was going to be a very special event. Instead of just doing Leaps of Joy or licking her ankles, I intended to throw myself into her arms, smother

her with doggly devotion, and lick every square inch of her face.

Then she would know for sure that . . . well, that I felt pretty bad about robbing her bird feeder and knocking it on the ground. And I did. I felt terrible about it. I was embarrassed, humiliated, and very very sorry . . . even though her scheming little cat had caused the whole thing.

No, wait. I wouldn't blame it on the cat this time. I had done it to myself. It was my own fault, and I would take full responsibility. I would make a confession, throw myself on her mercy, and let the chipmunks fall on the woodchucks.

She reached for the handle on the car door. I pushed the throttle lever up to Turbo Five. She opened the door. I fed the targeting information to Data Control and locked it into the computer.

Ten feet. Nine feet. Eight feet.

She turned and saw me coming and . . . yipes. Her face . . . I can't describe what happened to her face, but fellers, it went from being radiant and warm into an expression that sent cold chills down my backbone. I hit Full Air Brakes and came to a sliding stop.

In the dead silence, I beamed her a smile that said, "Hey, Sally May, great news. I'm here!"

She leveled a finger at me, and I mean like the

barrel of a gun, and hissed, *"Don't you even get close to me!"*

Huh?

Gee, what was the deal? I hadn't said anything. I hadn't done anything. I'd just gotten there.

She wrinkled her nose and puckered her mouth. "Where have you been? You smell like a dead horse . . . and YOU'RE GREEN!"

Green? Oh, yes, Emerald Pond, remember? Okay, sure, I'd been to the spa and that explained everything. She had caught the scent of my deep manly . . .

Just then, I noticed that the car door was hanging open. Hmm. Maybe she wanted me to ride into town with her. Hey, that made sense. I mean, she was probably in a hurry, and the ride into town would give us plenty of time to talk and share and patch things up.

I started toward the open door.

She shrank back. "Hank, get away! Loper, call your dog! If he jumps into my car, I'll murder him! I'm not kidding!"

Murder? Gee, that didn't sound good. I stopped in my tracks.

From the porch, Loper's voice boomed. "Hank, for crying out loud, get away!"

Sally May dived into the car and slammed the

door behind her, started the motor, and glared at me through the window glass. Her lips moved and she seemed to be saying something, but I couldn't make out her words.

I moved toward the car and delivered several barks that said, "I'll take care of the ranch while you're gone. And Sally May, I'll be right here when you get back!"

She rolled her window down a crack. "You are the most repulsive . . . STAY OUT OF THE SEWER!"

She went ripping away, spraying me with dirt and gravel. It left me with the impression that, well, our relationship still needed some work. Quite a lot of work.

Something about my smell had set her off. I mean, did you notice that she'd called me "repulsive"? That's pretty strong language, and it made me wonder . . . wait! I figured it out. *I hadn't spent enough time in Emerald Pond!* I hadn't given the waters enough time to do their magic. Those waters are powerful, but they need time to soak into every pore. Foolish me, I had done a quick in-and-out instead of . . .

But don't forget why I had gotten out so soon: birdseed. And the thought of birdseed sent my mind racing back to the little crook who had created this whole tragic situation. As the cloud of dust drifted away, I turned a murderous glare toward the yard . . . *and there he was.*

Pete. He was lounging in the iris patch, wearing that insolent smirk that drives me nuts. He batted his eyelids and waved.

Loper was still standing on the porch, so pounding the cat into rubble wasn't an option. Instead, I yelled out, "Pete, you're despicable!"

"I know, Hankie. How was the birdseed?"

"It was . . . Pete, you have a sick mind, and one of these days . . ."

"Yes?"

You know, I couldn't think of a good snappy reply. That happens sometimes, and it's really frustrating. You think of it two days later, when it doesn't do any good.

I whirled around and stormed away, holding my head at a proud angle. I hadn't won a clear moral victory over the little snake, but, by George, I could deprive him of my presence. If you think about it, that was pretty tough punishment, leaving the cat alone with himself. Nobody deserves Pete more than Pete.

I marched up the hill to the machine shed and headed straight toward the overturned Ford hubcap that held a fresh supply of . . . I know what you're thinking: I had spent quite a lot of time bad-mouthing Cheapo dog food and listing its shortcomings, but let me tell you something. The more you learn about bird food, the more you appreciate dog food, even the Cheapo Brand.

Yes, it was made out of garbage, but it was honest garbage. Yes, it was hard to chew, but once you ran it through the crusher and swallowed it down, it didn't send your body into convulsions. By George, once it landed in your stomach, it *stayed there*. No tricks, no surprises, just good honest American dog food.

Furthermore, if the folks at the feedstore needed a famous personality to plug the Cheapo Brand, they could use my name. How about this for a catchy little jingle they could print on the sack. "Try Cheapo. Good taste isn't everything." Or how about this one. "Buy Cheapo. Eating doesn't have to be fun."

Hey, do you suppose we could turn that into a song? I'm not sure. It'll be tough, but let's give it a shot. Here we go!

Eating Doesn't Have to Be Fun

Eating doesn't have to be fun.
It's something that we do to stay alive.

Dining isn't merely entertainment.
What we hope is to survive.

Cheapo dog food's hard as rock.
It's guaranteed to cause a shock,
Like chewing nails or oyster shell ...
It helps you to ignore the smell.

Our people never ask for our opinion
When they're shopping for our grub.
In fact, we'd rather have a kind of
    groceries
We can grind up without a club.

A sirloin steak would sure be nice,
But all they see's the bargain price.
If Cheapo's cheap, they'll buy a ton.
Look out, stomach, here it comes!

Oh well, there's more to life than what's
    for dinner.
We eat to live, not live to eat.
If Cheapo keeps the ranch from going
    bankrupt,
We'll just pretend that it's made of meat.

But that's a joke, we know it's not.
They make it out of all kinds of rot.

A loyal dog will never frown,
Just hold his nose and choke it down.

The future holds a lot of indigestion.
The stuff is bought and the deed is done . . .
But just remember
That eating doesn't have to be fun.

Pretty good, huh? You bet, and you know, I came up with it on the spur of the boot . . . the boot of the shovel . . . the rowel of the spur . . . the spur of the moment, there we go. It just popped into my head, and I think it turned out pretty well.

Anyway, I went to the overturned Ford hubcap and began . . . you know, the longer that stuff sits in a bowl, the harder it gets. It was pretty stiff. Rocks. Gravel. And even though it didn't taste so great . . . it tasted pretty bad. Petrified goat pellets.

It was awful! How could they sell this garbage? Yuck!

You know what the Cheapo motto ought to be? "Tired of your dog? Give him Cheapo! He'll move out."

Phooey. Maybe by tomorrow, I would be desperate enough to finish eating the stuff, but at the moment . . .

A chicken? A chicken was standing right beside

me, and all at once I noticed . . . well, drumsticks and Buffalo wings and pullybones. Hmmm.

No, wait, hold everything, stop, halt. It was a rooster. His name was J. T. Cluck and . . . well, we were more or less friends, so forget that I said anything about the . . . You-Know-Whats.

See, when you're hungry, it's hard to be friends with a chicken. No kidding. I mean, you talk about a moral struggle! Ranch dogs have to live with this twenty-four hours a day, and let me tell you, fellers, it's a test of inner strength and discipline. Some of us can handle the pressure and some of us, uh . . . how can I say this?

Okay, do you want to hear a deep, dark secret? I'm talking about the kind of secret that lurks in the deepest darkest dungeon of a dog's mind. It's the kind of secret we seldom share with the outside world, because . . . well, because it could get a dog in a world of trouble. But I'm going to reveal it. Here it is:

There isn't a ranch dog in the whole state of Texas that hasn't suffered a lapse in the Chicken Department.

Do you understand what that means? You know, it's probably better if you don't, because we're talking about . . . just forget that I brought it up. In fact, I didn't. I said nothing, almost nothing at all, about slurpens . . . chickens, that is, except that one was standing right beside me, and that's the honest truth.

Whew! This is a very touchy subject. I hope you understand.

No, I hope you *don't* understand. Let's skip it.

CHAPTER SIX

J. T. Cluck's
Report

Where were we? Oh yes. J. T. Cluck, the head rooster, had crept up behind me. He stood on one leg with his other leg pulled up under his wing, and he said, "Oh, here you are. I've been looking all over for you. I should have known you'd be eating . . . again."

"Again? What is that supposed to mean?"

"Well, seems like every time I look around, you've got your face stuck in that dog bowl."

"Yeah? Well, every time I look around, you're chasing bugs. I guess we all have to eat."

"Never thought about it that way." He craned his neck and peered into the bowl. "Is that stuff pretty good?"

"Try it yourself, be my guest."

"This ain't a trick, is it?"

"It's not a trick. I'm the kind of dog who doesn't mind sharing."

"Huh. Well, that's a new one. All right, maybe I'll give it a peck or two." He gave it two pecks. "It's kind of hard, ain't it?" He pecked again, really whammed it. He drew back his head, coughed, and spit it out. "You eat this stuff all the time?"

"Not all the time. It's a new brand, Cheapo."

"Well, it kind of explains your generosity." He laid a wing on my shoulder and winked. "It never hurts to be generous with slop, does it?"

I gave him a shove backward. "Is that the thanks I get for sharing my food with a chicken? Fine, skip it, sorry I bothered."

"Well, you don't need to get all hateful about it. All I meant was . . ." His eyes popped open, and he pounded his chest with a wing. "Uh-oh, here it comes."

I glanced around and saw nothing unusual. "Here *what* comes?"

"The galloping heartburn. I should have known."

I let out a groan. "Do I have to hear another story about your heartburn?"

"Well, no, I reckon you could leave, but if you stay around here, you're going to hear about it,

'cause when it hits, it hits hard." He bugged out his eyes and let out a ridiculous little chicken burp. "Yep, this is going to be a bad one, I can tell."

"Great."

"Elsa says I don't get enough gravel."

"Really? How is Elsa?"

"We need gravel for our gizzards, see, and when you don't get enough, it kind of backs things up."

"Boy, this weather has been nice."

"She thinks I need more gravel, but I think it's something else. If you ask me, there are certain kinds of food that set it off. You ever eat a spider?"

"No."

"Buddy, you talk about heartburn! One spider, and I mean even a little bitty one, will send you up in flames."

"J.T., I don't care."

"Huh?"

"I don't eat spiders, I don't get heartburn, and I don't care. Stop talking about heartburn."

He stared at me with his red rooster eyes. "Are you trying to tell me you never get indigestion?"

"That's correct. Never."

A nasty little grin spread across his beak. "Well, that's funny. What were you a-doing about twenty minutes ago, down by the sewer?"

"Have you been spying on me?"

He looked up at the sky and smirked. "Well, I keep my eyes open. Old J.T. sees a lot of things."

"Okay, I had indigestion, but it wasn't heartburn. I got poisoned by some birdseed."

He whipped his head around and stared at me. "Birdseed? Son, I could have told you that wouldn't work. A dog has no business eating bird food."

"I know that now, thanks."

"You ain't got a gizzard, see. It takes a good healthy gizzard to grind up all them little seeds. Heh. That was pretty dumb, you eating birdseed."

I pushed myself up on all fours. "Why do I bother talking to a chicken? You don't know anything, you never do anything, and all you can talk about is indigestion. I'm leaving, before I die of boredom."

"Now hold your horses. There's something important I need to tell you."

I stopped and turned back to him. "Not another heartburn story?"

"No sir, this is important, and it comes straight from Elsa."

"I'm listening."

He rubbed his chin with a wing. "Well, let me try to remember. You got me off on the wrong track."

"Hurry up. I'm a busy dog."

"Yeah, I've noticed. It's a wonder you ain't sprouted roots in that gunnysack bed."

"Hurry up!"

"I'm a-getting there, I'm a-getting there." He squinted one eye and stroked his chin. "Here we go. It was this morning, early. Elsa was pecking around them tall weeds west of the machine shed. They've got seeds this time of year, don't you know, and they're pretty tasty."

"What's the point?"

"Huh? The point? Well sir, the point is that she kind of strayed away from the chicken house. I've tried to warn her about that. I've told her, 'Honey, you stray too far and one of these times, a coyote's liable to jump out of them weeds and gobble you down.' But she don't listen. She's a wonderful hen but she's a little short on . . ." He tapped himself on the head.

"So what happened?"

"Well sir, there she was, pecking along in them weeds, when all of a sudden . . . she heard something."

"Yes?"

"Something very strange, and it put such a scare in her, she come back, flopping her wings and squawking to beat the band and running just as fast as an old fat hen can run. She come a-running up to me and she said, 'Oh, J.T., oh my, oh mercy me!'"

I waited for more. "Well? What was it?"

"It took me a while to get it out of her. She gets hysterical sometimes and can't hardly talk." He gazed off into the distance. "You know, her momma was that way, a fine woman but she took spells where all she could say was, 'Cluck, cluck, cluck!'"

"What did Elsa say?"

"Huh? Well, she said 'cluck' about fifty times."

"Is that all?"

"No sir, I finally got it out of her and . . ." He glanced over his shoulder and moved closer. "Pooch, this is liable to throw a scare into you. I want you to be ready for it."

"I'm ready, so hurry up."

"Well sir, what she heard was a whole army of coyotes out there in the wilderness—screeching and hollering and carrying on like I don't know what."

The word *coyotes* sent a shiver through my body. I moved closer. "Yes? Carrying on about what? Details, J.T., I need details."

He leaned closer. "Elsa said they were singing about . . . chickens."

"Chickens?"

"Yes sir, chickens, and you just won't believe the awful words! I'm not sure I should say 'em."

"Tell me, J.T. This could be important."

"All right. They said . . . here's exactly what they said . . . they said, 'Wishbone. Drumstick. Pullybone. Thigh.'"

Slurp. Suddenly, my, uh, tongue shot out of my mouth. "I see what you mean. That's shocking, all right."

He stared at me, twisting his head to the side. "Say, did you just lick your chops?"

"Me?" I turned away from him. "Don't be ridiculous. Go on with the story. Did Elsa get the impression that the coyotes were singing about food?"

"What do you think? Listen, pooch, a leg's a leg, but a drumstick's a piece of meat."

Slurp.

"Good point. So we have coyotes out in the pasture, singing about chicken dinners. That's not good. It could mean they're planning an attack on the chicken house."

"That's right, pooch, and our Defense Committee held a special meeting this very morning." He held himself erect. "We voted to take action."

"No kidding? What action?"

"Well sir, we all ran around in circles and

squawked for five minutes, twenty-seven hens and one rooster. It was something special."

I stared at him. "That was your *action*?"

"That's right. We planned to go on for ten minutes, but everybody got tired and we had to shut 'er down."

I laughed and shook my head. "Chickens. You ran around in circles and squawked for five minutes?"

"That's right, and now . . ." He stuck his beak in my face. "Mister, we want to know what *you're* going to do about it. I mean, when you ain't sleeping or eating bird food, you're supposed to be the guard dog around here."

I pushed his beak away. "I'm not at liberty to discuss my plans, but I can tell you this: I won't run around in circles and squawk."

"Well, that's probably good." He scowled. "You know, sometimes I ain't sure that squawking really helps, but it makes us feel like a team, you know what I'm saying? Team spirit's important."

For a moment, I was tempted to laugh in his face and tell him how dumb this sounded—team spirit among the chickens. But I didn't want to be rude, so I walked away. "J.T., I'll start an investigation and follow the usual procedures. I may have some more questions, so don't leave town."

He called out one last gem of chicken wisdom. "Well, that'll be easy, mister, seeing as how we ain't got a town. We live in the *country,* in case you didn't notice."

"Great point, J.T. Don't speak to any coyotes."

I chuckled all the way down to the office. What a birdbrain!

CHAPTER SEVEN

A Serious Case
of Worms

I rode the elevator up to the twelfth floor and
went striding into the office, checked the mail
and glanced over a few reports on my desk, then
flopped down on my gunnysack bed.

Only then did I notice Drover. He was lying on
his stomach, with both paws out in front and his
head pointed straight ahead. Suddenly it struck
me that he looked exactly like the statue of the
Great Squink in . . . wherever that ancient monument
resides . . . Messitallupia . . . Pottamotamia . . .
Agrippa . . . Eejippum . . . Egypt, there we go.

Let's back up and put it all together again. He
looked exactly like that famous statue in some
distant land beyond the seashells. It appeared
that he hadn't moved a hair while I'd been gone.

His eyes swung around. "Oh, hi. What's going on?"

"I've been out taking care of ranch business."

"I'll be derned. How's business?"

"Business is mixed. My main objective was to patch up my relationship with Sally May, and that sort of blew up in my face."

With dreamy eyes, he stared off in the distance with dreamy eyes. "Yeah, I've always liked blue. It's my favorite color. Blue sky, blue ocean water . . ."

"Hey, did you hear what I said?"

He squinted and looked closer at me. "Oh, hi. Did you say something?"

"Yes, and I'd appreciate it if you would pay attention. I said, my mission to patch up my relationship with Sally May *blew up* in my face." I heaved a sigh. "Drover, the woman is impossible. What does a dog have to do to please her?"

"Oh . . . stay out of the sewer, I guess."

"I rushed down to wish her a safe journey. I was ready to heal old wounds . . . what did you say?"

"Stay out of the sewer. You stink."

I leaped to my feet and towered over him. "Why you little . . . how dare you make slanderous remarks about your commanding officer? Have you forgotten who I am? How would you like to stand with your nose in the corner for five years, huh?"

"Hank, you stink and she hates the sewer smell. I tried to tell you."

"Drover, that is the most outrageous . . ." My mind raced back to the scene with Sally May. "Wait a second. She did say something about the sewer . . . and my smell." I sank back into my gunnysack. "You tried to tell me?"

"Yeah, but you never listen."

"But why didn't you just come out and say that?"

"I don't know, 'cause you never listen, I guess."

There was a long throbbing moment of silence. "Drover, we've been through a lot together. May I speak frankly?"

"Oh sure, you bet. My life's an open book."

"Drover, sometimes I feel that . . . what's the word I'm searching for?"

"Bonehead?"

"No. Sometimes I feel that I don't listen very well."

"I'll be derned."

"It's as though . . . well, I get so wrapped up in the big picture that I don't pay attention to the little picture."

"Yeah, and a picture is worth a thousand worms."

"Exactly. Drover, I think I've got worms.

They're affecting my memory, my ability to hear, my ability to listen."

"Yeah, those worms are bad. Maybe you got 'em from the birdseed."

I leaped to my feet and began pacing, as I often do when my mind is racing. "That's it! You've hit the nail right on the hammer. It's common knowledge that birdseed is a major source of parasites."

"I've always wanted to see Paris."

"And what is the most common type of parasite?"

"Oh, most of 'em are Frenchmen, I guess."

"Worms, Drover, a dangerous kind of internal parasite."

"You know, the site I'd like to see is the Rifle Tower."

I whirled around and faced him. "So there we have it. I suffer from attention lapses because *I have worms*. Quick, to the sewer! I must heal myself!"

I rushed out of the office, went flying down twelve flights of stairs, ran through the lobby with all its hanging chandeliers and paintings of famous dogs, sprinted all the way to Emerald Pond, and launched myself into its warm embrace.

As the waters closed around me, I felt a tingling sensation all over my body. I knew the elixirs were elixing and the tonics were tonicking, as the waters began curing my case of worms and healing my gizzardly depths.

By the time Drover arrived, huffing and puffing, I was feeling much better. "Drover, I'm healed! I feel more like myself right now than I ever have in my whole life."

"Yeah, and you'll smell even worse."

"The worms are gone. I've got my hearing back. I can hear you as though you're standing right there in front of me."

"Yeah, 'cause I am."

I waded out to the shore and gave myself a vigorous shake, sending a spray of fragrant drops in all directions. Drover cringed and backed away because, well, because he hates water. That's another part of his weirdness.

After shaking, I scratched up dirt and rolled around in it, kicking all four legs in the air, then leaped to my feet, and shook one last time. "Look closely, Drover. Standing before you is a new dog."

"Yeah, Sally May's really going to be proud."

"Indeed she will." I marched over to him and laid a paw on his shoulder. "And Drover, we must give you some credit. You're the one who discovered the link between the birdseed and my hearing

67

loss. Worms!" I noticed that he was backing away from me and making a sour face. "What's wrong?"

"Something just happened to the air."

"Really?" I glanced around at the air. "Oh yes, I see what you mean. It's become almost invisible, but don't be alarmed. Air is supposed to be invisible, so all is well."

"No, it smells like a dead horse."

"A dead horse? Hmmm. You know, Sally May said the same thing. We'd better do an inventory of the horses. We might have lost one." Drover fell to the ground and covered his ears with his paws. I rushed to his side. "What happened?"

He let out a moan. "You never listen. You never hear anything!"

"Drover, the reason you can't hear anything is that your ears are covered. You can't go through life with your ears plugged."

"I can't stand anymore!"

"Drover, uncover your ears, and that's a direct order!"

He didn't move, so I had to take matters into my own hands. The little guy needed help. I pried one of his paws away from his ear and gave him a blast of Train Horns. BWONK! It had an electrifying effect. His eyes popped open, and he sprang three feet straight up. His ears were flapping, and he appeared to be swimming through the air, moving four paws and two ears at the same time.

He made quite a sight and, heh heh, I must admit that I kind of enjoy doing Train Horns. It's more fun with a cat, but Drover always puts on a good show.

He hit the ground with a thud, and I rushed over to him. "There, is that better?"

"Better than what?"

"Good! You can hear me now. Stand up, I have a presentation to make." He wobbled up to a standing position, and I noticed that his eyes were crossed. "Please don't cross your eyes. This is a solemn occasion."

"I can't help it. You never listen. It makes me crazy."

"Drover, what makes you crazy is that you plug your ears and cross your eyes. It's not normal. Now, stand up straight. I'm going to give you an award."

His eyes came into focus and he grinned. "An award, no fooling?"

"Yes. You're the one who found the mysterious link between birdseed and my hearing loss. It was a brilliant piece of detective work. Thanks to you, I can hear again."

"Yeah, but you still don't listen."

"Exactly, and as a way of showing my gertrude, I'm going to give you a promotion."

He beamed with pride and began wiggling his stub tail. "Gosh, no fooling?"

"Yes, I'm promoting you to First Scout."

"First Scout, oh goodie. I've always wanted to be a scout."

"And I'm sending you out on a very important assignment."

His smile froze. "Assignment?"

"See, we think there might be some trouble brewing with the coyotes. We've gotten a report . . ."

THUD! He hit the ground like a rock.

Drover Cheats

The little guy was rolling around on the ground and obviously in some kind of pain. "Good grief, now what?"

"Drat the luck, this old leg just quit me!"

"Drover, I'm trying to give you an award. This promotion could be very important to your career."

"I know, but I can't get my career off the ground when my leg doesn't work. Oh, my leg!"

"Are you saying you can't go on this mission?"

"Oh no, I'd never say that. I've got to do it . . . for the ranch!"

"That's the spirit."

He made a valiant attempt to regain his feet, jacking himself off the ground, one leg at a time.

But once he'd made it up on all fours, he fell over like a bicycle. BAM!

"Oh, the pain! Maybe you'd better go without me."

"Actually, I hadn't planned on going. We'll need someone here at headquarters to, uh, handle communications."

"Hey, that's the job for me."

"It's *not* the job for you. All this electronic gear is very complicated. You'd probably stick your nose into a socket and get yourself fried. No, we can't risk leaving you here. It would be too dangerous. I think you would be much happier, going out into the wilderness to spy on the cannibals."

I waited for him to shake off his pain, leap to his feet, and start the mission. He didn't move. I heaved a sigh and paced a few steps away. "All right, Drover, let's try the path of negotiation. What would it take to sweeten the deal? Let's talk bonus, incentives, benefits . . . what would it take?"

"Gosh, I don't know. Let me think here." He sat up and went into a moment of deep concentration. "Anything?"

"Anything within reason."

He gave it another minute of thought, then beamed a smile. "Just grant me one little wish."

"Not a big one?"

"Nope, it's tee-eency. You'll hardly even notice it."

"Hmmm." I marched over to him and looked him straight in the eyes. "All right, I'll grant you one tiny wish, and we'll seal it with our Cowdog Oaths. What's your tiny wish?"

"My tiny wish is . . ." He rolled his eyes up to the clouds. "I wish that you'd go on this mission and leave me here, 'cause my leg's killing me."

His words went through me like a jolt of lightning, starting just behind my ears, moving down my spine, and going all the way to the end of my tail. Speechless, I stared at the runt. I couldn't believe he'd done this to me!

"Drover, that's cheating!"

"Yeah, but we made a deal."

"It's a low-down cheating deal. It's trickery, it's the kind of underhanded swindle I would expect from a cat but not from you!" I paced several steps away. "Drover, we could always renegotiate."

"No thanks."

"We could have a cooling-off period, then come back to the table. What do you say?"

"You gave your Cowdog Oath."

"I know that, but . . ." I marched back to him and screamed in his face. "Don't you understand? This could be a very dangerous mission! Do you actually want to put your commanding officer in harm's way?" He didn't answer. I was snookered. "All right, you little crook, I'll take the mission, but this will go into your Permanent Record!" I whirled around and stalked away. "I have nothing more to say to you."

"I never thought I'd see the day."

"What?"

"I said, I hope you have a nice day."

"I will *not* have a nice day, and don't tell me what to do."

"Well, have a terrible day."

"I will." I did an about-face and went back to him. "Here's an idea. How about Scrap Rights? See, we could throw two or three days' of Scrap Rights into the deal and . . ." He was shaking his head. "Like I said, there's no future in trying to reason with a crook, and that's what you are, Drover, a miserable little crook. Good-bye."

I whirled around and marched away, leaving the little mutter-mumble to stew in his own tomatoes. Fine. I would do the mission. I thrive on tough assignments, and the tougher the better. When you get to be Head of Ranch Security, you take the bitter with the sour and make lemonade out of the pickles.

With my head held high, I marched away from

home and gunnysack, away from comfort and leisure and all the other things that had corrupted Drover and turned him into the kind of pampered little weenie I had never wanted to be. I was pumped and ready to tackle this new assignment, and the excitement of doing battle with the entire coyote nation filled me with . . .

You know what? It filled me with DREAD, is what it filled me with, and by the time I reached the machine shed, I was, uh, having second thoughts. And third and fourth thoughts. I did a quick glance in all directions (nobody was watching) and darted inside.

Well, why not? If the coyotes raided the chicken house, so what? Did I care about chickens? No. They weren't my chickens. All at once, a feeling of peace and tranquittery washed over my mind. It was clear what we needed to do at this point in the investigation: hide in the machine shed and, you know, give things a chance to work themselves out.

Planning. We needed to develop a detailed plan, see, and the machine shed offered the kind of quiet atmosphere that was perfect for long-range planning. If the coyotes launched a raid, I would be in position to observe it through a peephole. Just think of all the valuable information I could gather about their troop strength and tactics. Great information.

So, yes, this was the time to lay low and regroup in the machine shed. Don't forget, this was Drover's Secret Sanctuary, the place where he sought refuge from Life and all its complications. If it worked for Drover, by George, it might work for me, too.

And so it was that I slithered my way into the backest, darkest, dustiest corner of the machine shed, into the gloomy depths where Sally May stored her grandmother's antique furniture and Loper stored his canvas-covered canoe. There in the silence, I found peace and quiet, and felt not one shred of guilt.

Okay, let's be honest. I felt some guilt, but I could handle it. No one would ever find me here. No one would ever . . .

"Hey pooch, come out of there!"

Huh? Unless my ears were playing tricks on me, I had just heard a voice, perhaps the voice of a meddling rooster. But that was impossible. I was hidden, invisible to enemy radar. I sank lower into the gloomy shadows.

"Pooch, I saw you go in there, so you might as well come out."

Disguising my voice, I called out, "We have no dogs in here. Go away."

"Well, if you ain't a dog, what are you?"

"I'm . . . I'm the troll of the machine shed."

"Oh yeah? I don't believe in trolls."

"Well, I don't believe in roosters. Go away."

"How'd you know I'm a rooster?"

I flinched. "It was a wild guess."

"Heh. You just got mousetrapped, pooch. Are you coming out or do you want me to come in there and root you out?"

Oh brother. I had been exposed. I pushed myself up to a standing position and headed for the slot of light between the big sliding doors. There, a long-tailed, red-eyed rooster stood in the gap between the doors, peering inside and wearing a haughty little smirk. Just as I had suspected, it was J. T. Cluck.

I paced up to him and gave him an unfriendly glare. "You didn't see me come in here. I checked, and you were nowhere around."

He chuckled. "Yeah, it was a shot in the dark, all right, but I smoked you out, didn't I? Caught you hiding, didn't I? Heh heh."

"You didn't catch me, and I'm not hiding."

"Then what were you doing in there, huh?"

"For your information, I was going over reports

and planning my schedule for the rest of the month."

"Yeah, I'll bet."

"What do you want? I'm busy and I don't wish to be disturbed."

He leaned toward me. "Well, too bad, 'cause you're fixing to be disturbed. Them coyotes are howling again, and I want you to hear it."

"J.T., we've been studying Elsa's report about the coyotes and we've decided . . ."

"Come on, dog, this ain't Elsa talking. This is the real thing."

I didn't want to get involved in this chicken business, but there was a note of urgency in his voice. I left the barn and followed J.T. Little did I know . . . well, you'll see.

Pullybones and
Drumsticks

I followed J. T. Cluck around to the west side of the machine shed. There, to my surprise, I saw twenty-seven white leghorn hens huddled in a group. They weren't clucking or making a sound, and that struck me as odd. Under normal conditions, our barnyard chickens would be making some kind of noise, but these weren't. They seemed to be looking off to the north, toward the big canyons in the distance.

When they heard us approaching, they turned and stared at me with worried eyes, as though the dummies thought I had ... *slurp* ... evil intentions or something ridiculous like that. J.T. must have noticed their concern and said, "Y'all don't fret.

He's the guard dog around here. I want him to hear this. Are they still carrying on out there?"

The chickens nodded, and several pointed their wings to the north. They cocked their heads and listened. I lifted my right ear to the Full Gathering Position and swung it around to the north. At first I heard only a whisper of wind, but then . . . *there it was,* a very strange sound. I mean, it gave me the creeps.

Should I describe it? I guess we can give it a try. Here's exactly what I heard, a rumble of menacing voices, chanting these words:

> Wishbone!
> Drumstick!
> Pullybone!
> Thigh, thigh!
>
> Wishbone!
> Drumstick!
> Pullybone!
> Thigh, thigh!

J.T. swung his gaze around to me. "What do you say now, pooch?"

"I'd say those are coyotes, maybe eight or ten of them, and they've got mischief on their minds. I mean, when they start chanting about . . .

slurp . . . drumsticks and all those other bodily parts, they're up to no good."

"That's right, and now you know I didn't make it up." He cocked his head and locked one of his rooster eyes on me. "Say, you've got water dripping off your tongue. What's the deal, you got hydrophobia or something?"

I turned my back on him so that he couldn't see . . . so that he wouldn't be distracted by, uh, distractions. "J.T., could we stick to the point?"

"Well, if you'll quit dripping, I'll quit worrying about it. It don't look healthy."

I mopped up the water inside my mouth and whirled around. "J.T., the coyotes are getting worked up to raid the chicken house. Sally May wouldn't like that."

J.T. rocked up and down on his toes. "I told you that an hour ago. What are you going to do about it?"

My mind was racing. "Somebody needs to go out there and check it out, and I was thinking . . . well, maybe you'd like to volunteer."

"Heh heh. Nope. You're the big dog around here. Saddle up, son, and do your duty. While you're gone, me and the girls will make some preparations of our own. Good luck . . . and don't go running any rabbits out there." He turned to the hens. "All right, y'all, gather around. There's danger lurking, and we're fixing to go into our Disaster Drill. Ready? Go!"

You'd have thought a stick of dynamite had gone off in the middle of those chickens. There was an explosion of squawks and flapping wings, and suddenly hysterical birds were running around in all directions, shrieking, "Disaster! Help! Run! Earthquake! Fire! Murder! The sky is falling!"

It was crazy, but exactly the sort of behavior you can expect from a bunch of brainless birds. If I hadn't moved out of the way, they would have run smooth over the top of me. Does that make any sense? I got paid for protecting these morons, but there they were . . . oh well.

I left the riot of screeching birds and headed north in a long trot. I wasn't looking forward to this. I'd had plenty of experience in dealing with the savages, and most of it had been unpleasant.

See, coyotes look like dogs, and they can bark like dogs, and sometimes they act like dogs, but they're *not* dogs. Now, if a guy happened to catch Rip and Snort on a good day, he could have some fun. They loved to sing, wrestle, roll on dead skunks, fight badgers, and hold belching contests, and I'd had some good laughs with them.

They were good old boys, but they had a nasty

FIRE
THE SKY IS FALLING
MURDER
EARTHQUAKE
FIRE
DISASTER
RUN
HELP
RUN
FIRE
RUN
RUN
DISASTER
RUN

habit of changing into *bad* old boys, and it could happen before you knew it. When their yellow eyes started to glitter with unholy light, when you saw their teeth catching the glint of the sun, you knew it was time to head back to the house . . . fast.

And then there was Scraunch the Terrible. Scraunch had never made any pretense of being a good old boy. He was bad to the bone. He was born bad, and he'd devoted all his energy into staying that way. I knew the guy pretty well. He loved chicken dinners, and he hated ranch dogs. As you might guess, Scraunch and I had never gotten along very well.

Oh, and there was one more awkward detail in my dealings with Scraunch. He had a beautiful sister and . . . well, let's just say that when Missy Coyote and I looked into each other's eyes, sparks of love flew in all directions. If Scraunch happened to be around, that made it, uh, very awkward.

See, a dog should never fall in love with a cannibal's sister. I knew that. I knew it was The Love That Could Never Be, but . . . well, a guy can't always control his emotions, even if he's Head of Ranch Security.

Ah, sweet Missy, coyote princess of my dreams! The very mention of her name caused my head to spin with delicious thoughts . . . dangerous thoughts.

But I couldn't allow myself to dwell on romance. I had a job to do. I was on a mission, and I sure didn't need . . . boy, she was pretty, had the nicest coat of hair you ever saw . . . I sure didn't need any distractions.

Anyway, it was time to concentrate. Job. Duty. Discipline.

I headed north up a sand draw, moving at a brisk pace toward the sound of drumming and chanting. It seemed to be coming from an area near the mouth of a deep canyon, one of those dark places that . . . *gulp* . . . make a dog think that he doesn't belong there. We're talking about a wild and spooky place, home to the cannibals.

This was crazy! Why was I doing this? To protect a bunch of featherbrained chickens? I didn't care about the chickens! *Slurp.* In fact . . . never mind.

Sally May. I was doing it for Sally May, to mend our broken relationship.

On and onward I pushed myself, deeper and deeper into a wild and strange land where no dog should venture alone. But fellers, I *was* alone. I had never felt aloner in my whole life.

The coyote voices were getting louder now. I

slowed to a walk and crept toward a line of cedar trees. There, I parted the branches and gazed down into the ravine below. What I saw caused my breath to catch in my throat, and I think my heart even stopped beating.

Yipes. It was the coyotes, all right, seven of them, and they appeared to be getting themselves tuned up for some serious mischief. Remember that, back at the ranch, I'd heard the faint sound of chanting? Well, this was the source of it—seven bloodthirsty cannibals hopping around in a big circle and yelling at the top of their lungs. Here, listen to this.

The Coyote Chicken Chant

Chicken, git the chicken, git the chicken
    chicken!
Chicken, git the chicken, git the chicken
    chicken!

Wishbone!
Drumstick!
Pullybone!
Thigh, thigh!

Wishbone!

Drumstick!
Pullybone!
Thigh, thigh!

Yum yum, eat 'em up, eat 'em up.
Yum yum, eat 'em up, eat 'em up.

Is that weird or what? It was one of the weirdest things I'd seen and heard in my whole career. I mean, they were doing it in perfect rhythm and all the parts fit together, so that it had a kind of a hypnopotomizing effect . . . hypnotizing effect, let us say. I mean, the words and the rhythm . . . the chanting and drums . . . they all blended together and got inside my head and . . .

Slurp.

Slurp, slurp, slurp.

I kind of hate to reveal this next part. In fact, I'm not going to. Why should I pass along a report about me . . . well, going off the deep end, losing touch with Reality, slipping the leash of civilization, and going AWOL? I shouldn't report it. There's nothing in it for me but trouble, and who needs that?

Nothing happened, okay? I didn't actually see the coyotes doing what I said they were doing. In fact, I didn't see any coyotes. I saw nothing, almost nothing at all.

All right, maybe I saw something, but it turned out to be . . . ha ha . . . you won't believe this, but those creatures turned out to be *prairie dogs*. No kidding. Ha ha. Seven or eight fat little prairie dogs, running around in circles and chanting:

> Green grass!
> Weed seeds!
> Grass roots!
> Dig a hole, dig a hole!

Sounds pretty cute, doesn't it? You bet. They were precious, seven little guys playing in the pasture and having some prairie dog fun. Ha ha. And there was nothing about their actions that made you think of . . . well, chicken dinners *slurp* or antisocial behavior or raids on chicken houses, nothing wild or crazy. Honest.

So there isn't much to report and what do you say we, uh, rewind the story and go back to my conversation with J. T. Cluck in the machine shed? Will that be all right? Good. Stand by for Story Rewind.

Click, whir, gibble, geek, squeak, squiggle.

Okay, we have completed the Story Rewind Procedure, and we're back in front of the machine shed. Over here on the right, you see J. T. Cluck, the head rooster, and over on the left . . . hey, that's me! This modern technology is pretty neat, isn't it? I mean, it allows us to cut and paste our experiences and to delete the little snippets that are . . . well, unpleasant or embarrassing.

So there we are, J.T. and I. He tells me that he's been hearing coyotes howling in the pasture, something about drumsticks and pullybones . . . *slurp* . . . ha ha . . . and I tell him, "J.T., you've been dreaming. I don't believe one word of that yarn. It's probably just a bunch of prairie dogs."

And that's about all, no kidding. Nothing else happened that day and, gee, I guess we've come to the end of the story.

Ha ha ha.

Ha ha.

Ha.

Wait! Don't leave. There's more.

CHAPTER TEN

The Darkness in
a Dog's Mind

Remember what we said about modern technology? It allows us to edit our work, so to speak, and to cut out the parts we don't like? It gives us the opportunity to retell old stories and to give them whatever shape we want.

But you know what? That's just a fancy name for LYING. You don't cut, paste, edit, or delete the Truth. Truth isn't a word or a blip on a tape. It's something that defines who you are. If you tell the truth, you're an honest dog. If you don't, you're a dishonest skunk.

And fellers, that's not me.

Oh brother. I didn't want to finish this story. You're going to be disappointed in me. You're going to think . . . but never mind. Let's get it over with.

Grab hold of something solid.

Sigh.

Okay, remember what we said about the darkness in a dog's mind? Well, there are dark and spooky parts in a dog's mind, and in the very darkest rooms, you will find visions of . . . ROASTED CHICKEN ON A PLATE.

There it is. Ranch dogs get paid for guarding the chickens, but we live in a constant state of torment because . . . WE WANT TO EAT THEM!! Did you happen to notice all those "slurps" that have been creeping into my conversations? Well, they didn't get there by accident. They popped up because . . . this is very difficult . . . because the word "chicken" *causes my mouth to water*!

Why? I don't know. It's not my idea. I don't want to go around thinking about chicken dinners. I have a respectable job. I want to be a good dog. It just happens. And there's more. If you want to get a dog seriously stirred up, all you have to do is say, *"Chicken, git the chicken, git the chicken chicken!"* That will push him over the edge and turn him into a raving lunatic.

There it is, the Ugly Truth. After listening to the cannibals for two minutes, I had gone over the edge—not sliding over the edge but crashing, head over heels, down into the darkness where ranch dogs should never go.

I told you that you'd be disappointed. Sorry. I tried to avoid this, I didn't want to reveal it, but . . . let's get on with it.

Something snapped inside my mind. Water poured through my mouth like a raging river. My eyeballs turned in circles, and I heard thirteen cuckoo clocks going off inside my head: "Cuckoo, cuckoo, cuckoo!"

Before I knew what was happening, I let out a blood-chilling howl, leaped out from behind the cedar trees, and yelled, "Wait for me, I want to join up!" I went tearing down the embankment and joined the circle of cannibals.

They were . . . well, pretty shocked to see me. Very shocked. The music (or whatever it was) stopped. The dancing and yelling stopped, and seven pairs of yellow coyote eyes turned to me as I cried out, "Hey guys, in my secret heart, I've always wanted to be a cannibal and here I am!"

I had hoped they might . . . well, burst into a chorus of cheers or at least applaud. They didn't. This should have served as a warning, but I wasn't exactly in my right mind. See, once you get chicken in your head, common sense packs its bags and moves out.

The coyotes exchanged puzzled glances, then Snort stepped forward. "That you, Hunk? Same ranch dog we know before?"

"That's right, pal, only things are different now. I quit my job, see. I'm just one of the boys."

"Hunk not guard ranch no more? Not protecting chicken house?"

"No sir. I heard your song and, well, it has changed my life. I'm ready to join up. What a deal, huh? You bet. So . . . well, let's go get a chicken dinner. What are we waiting for?"

Nobody moved and all eyes turned in the same direction, toward . . . yipes! You know, in all the excitement, I had almost forgotten how big and ugly Scraunch was, but now it all came crashing back like two hundred plates hitting a cement floor.

The guy was HUGE, a full head taller than the other coyotes. He had scars on his face and notches bitten out of his ears, long gleaming teeth, and a pair of red-rimmed eyes that could scorch the bark off a tree.

He stepped out of the circle and came toward me. *Thump, thump, thump.* The others shrank back and cleared a path for him. There wasn't a sound

95

to be heard . . . actually, there were several sounds: his footsteps and my knees knocking together.

Gulp. Maybe this hadn't been such a great idea.

He walked a circle around me, sizing me up. He stopped and fixed me in the blaze of his unblinking yellow eyes. Then in a menacing growl, he said, "Hunk berry foolish for leave house and boom-boom."

I struggled to find my voice. "Yes, well, it was kind of a sudden impulse. See, I came out here to spy on you guys, but then I heard your song and all at once I thought, gee, wouldn't it be fun to be a coyote! No job or responsibilities, sleep all day then go out and bump off a few chickens. Hey, what a life! Anyway, here I am, ready or not. Ha ha."

No one laughed or even smiled. They just stared.

I felt the need to keep talking. "See, ranch dogs aren't allowed to eat chickens, but if I join up with you guys . . ."

Scraunch held up his paw for silence. "Hunk shut trap."

"Shut my trap? Well, I guess I could, but let me hasten to point out . . ."

He clamped my jaws shut and turned to the other coyotes. "Coyote Brotherhood hold big vote on whichsomever to eat, chickens or ranch dog!"

What! A *vote on whether to eat chickens or me?* Hey, I'd just gotten there. What kind of deal was this? I tried to express my opinions on this, but Scraunch had a pretty good grip on my muzzle, and all I could say was, "Mum mum mutt mutter."

Scraunch continued. "Whosomever wanting to eat chicken, raise right paw!" The coyotes glanced around. No one raised a paw and, well, that made me uneasy. But then Snort raised his left paw (he'd always had trouble with left and right, if you recall) and one by one, the others did the same, until all six of them were holding up their left paws.

Good! They had all voted *not* to eat me.

Scraunch released his grip on my face and started counting the votes. "One. Four. Tuesday-three. Drop paws!" The coyotes lowered their paws. "Now, whosomever wanting to eat ranch dog, raise right foot!"

Scraunch was the only one who lifted his paw.

Whew! Boy, I'd been pretty worried there for a minute. I mean, you never know how an election's going to turn out. Just when you think you're doing well in the polls, you get a nasty surprise. Voters are friggle.

Voters are frugal.

Voters are sniggle.

You know, there's a word that describes the nature of voters, suggesting that they often change their minds at the last moment. It's the perfect word for this situation, but I can't remember it.

Voters are frickle . . . freckle . . . speckled . . .

Wait. Voters are FICKLE, there we go. See, it was the perfect word. Voters are fickle, and you can never be sure until the last moment which way the election is going to turn, and this is especially true in coyote elections. I mean, those guys are . . . well, they're dumber than dirt, might as well go right to the point, so you never know.

But it appeared that I had won the election and figured it was time for me to, well, deliver a speech.

I faced the electorate with a broad smile. "Guys, this is a great day for me. As a pup, I always dreamed of running away from home and becoming a cannibal. There's just something about your way of life that strikes a chord in the mind of an impressionable young dog. You're probably wondering what it is."

They just sat there, staring at me with empty eyes. No smiles, no frowns, no expression at all. It almost made me think that . . . well, they weren't interested in my speech, but who could believe that? I mean, this was a very special moment, and I had an important message to share with them.

I plunged on with the speech. "You know what it is? I'll tell you. The part of your culture that appeals to young dogs all over the world is . . . *you're totally worthless*. I mean, what a great life you have out here in the wilderness! You're all bums! You never work or contribute anything to the good of the world. You sleep all day, get up at sundown, howl at the moon, scratch a few fleas, then go out, get sprayed by skunks, fight badgers, beat up bobcats . . .

"Fellers, you have set the standard for young dogs all over the world. Your singing is legendary, and I don't need to tell you that your Chicken Chant is one of the most moving pieces I've ever heard. Before I got here, I was a normal dog. Now . . . I stand before you, a changed dog, a chicken maniac to the core. What a great influence you're having in this world!"

I filled my tanks with air and moved on to the conclusion of my speech. "Gentlemen, friends, distinguished guests . . . I want to thank you for your vote of confidence. For years, you've been an inspiration to dogs all over Texas. Tomorrow and next week and next month, when I meet a young dog who has dreams of being a bum, I'll tell him to study the example of our coyote brothers who have raised bumhood to a science. I'll tell him . . ."

All at once, I noticed my audience had . . . well, they appeared to have fallen asleep. I mean, they were slumped against each other like sacks of feed, snoring, wheezing, flapping their lips. Gee, I had gotten so carried away with my speech, I hadn't noticed. Maybe I needed to raise my voice, but before I could continue, Scraunch tapped me on the shoulder.

I turned and saw that he had brought a paw to his lips, and he said, "Shhhh." Then he faced the unconscious brotherhood and yelled, "Hey!" Six sleeping cannibals flinched and opened their eyes.

Snort glanced around and leaped to his feet. "Snort change vote. Never mind chicken. Eat dog!"

The others grumbled, exchanged glances, and nodded their heads. I was stunned and turned to Snort. "Hey, you can't do that! I won the election, fair and square."

Snort nodded. "Hunk talk too much, put coyotes to sleep with yap-yap. Coyotes eat Hunk to shut him up!"

"Snort, you cast your vote. If you change it now . . . well, that would be cheating." I whirled around to Scraunch. "Scraunch, they're trying to steal the election!"

I said this, hoping to shame them. Well, that flopped. All seven coyotes roared with wicked laughter, and Scraunch whopped me on the back. "Ha! Coyote cheat all the time, love to cheat even moresomever than eat chicken. Ho ho!"

"Yes, but . . . Scraunch, this is an outrage. I just delivered a very emotional speech that paid tribute to Cannibal Culture. Okay, maybe it went a little too long, but would you actually eat me for that?"

I held my breath and waited for his answer. Scraunch nodded. Snort nodded. His brother Rip nodded. All of them nodded.

Gulp.

Fellers, it appeared that I had walked into a bear trap and had gotten myself into the kind of mess that has no happy ending.

Thrown in a Coyote Dungeon

Well, when a brave ranch dog finds himself in an unsniggable situation, he has only two options: fight or run. Naturally, my first thought was to go down swinging.

But then I took a closer look at Scraunch, that oak tree of pure meanness towering over me, staring at me with terrible eyes, grinning, and licking his chops . . . and, well, that sort of narrowed my options down to one. I would have to rely on my amazing speed, go to Full Turbos, and race the entire coyote nation back to the ranch.

Just as I was reaching for the throttle, I felt myself being jerked off the ground and hoisted up on the shoulders of several muscular cannibals, who seemed to be pretty serious about kidnapping me and carrying me back to the coyote village—where, I surmised, they planned to eat me for supper.

I tried to register a protest. "Scraunch, this is an outrage! I demand a hearing. Dogs have rights, too!"

This brought forth a chorus of rowdy laughter, hoots, snickers, and other sounds of mockery. I tried another approach.

"Snort, think of all the good times we've had. Remember the day we rolled on the dead skunk and sang 'Rotten Meat'? Remember that? Those were happy times, Snort. Don't throw them all away."

More irreverent laughter.

"Okay, we're getting down to the bottom of the list. Let's talk about the Brotherhood of All Animals. You know, we're very similar, dogs and coyotes. Think about it, guys: four paws, one tail, two ears, two eyes, hairy legs. We're pretty close to the same, and it's even been said that we're kinfolks. I'm sure you'll agree that it would be terrible manners to eat your kinfolks, right? Talk to me, guys."

"Hunk shut trap!"

"All right, let's try a different approach."

"Hunk shut trap!

Well, that kind of killed the conversation. When they keep telling you to shut your trap, you begin to think that nobody is listening. There was nothing left for me to do but sit back and enjoy the ride, only I didn't enjoy the ride. Who can enjoy a ride that's taking him to a village full of cannibals? Yikes.

We got there a lot sooner than I wished. The coyote village was located up in one of those deep dark canyons. There wasn't much to the village, just holes in the ground, caves in the canyon wall, and a bunch of bleached bones spread out over half an acre.

You talk about something that will shake your confidence. Try *half an acre of bleached bones*.

As we tramped into the village, other coyotes came pouring out of holes and caves, yelling and cheering. One of the first to reach us was an old, shriveled, moth-eaten coyote who walked with a limp . . . or maybe two limps. He was pretty crippled up, and I knew the guy. It was Chief Many Rabbit Gut Eat In Full Moon, the father of Scraunch and Missy.

I'd met him before on another occasion and he'd seemed pretty friendly . . . in a creepy cannibal sort of way, of course. I'd gotten the feeling that he liked me and that we could talk, man to man.

He rushed up and gave me a big smile. "Aha, ranch dog come back to coyote billage!"

"Hi, Chief, great to see you again. Listen, you need to talk to your men. We've had a little misunderstanding. See, I came to join up and, you know, poach a chicken or two. I think I could make a contribution, no kidding."

The old man nodded and widened his grin. "Hunk make big contribution. Hunk make supper, oh boy!"

Well, there went another idea down in flames, and I didn't have many ideas left . . . only one. I ran my eyes over the crowd, hoping to find Missy Coyote. Remember Missy? She had helped me escape her bloodthirsty relatives on several occasions, and I felt pretty confident that she would save me one more time. Good old Missy!

I searched the crowd . . . and my heart began to sink. She wasn't there! Gulp. Missy had been my last hope and now . . .

Gulp.

The whole population of the village seemed excited to see me, but I knew it had nothing to do with my charm, personality, good looks, or winning smile. No, they celebrated my coming for all the wrong reasons, and it certainly appeared that my time was running out.

Scraunch and his friends tossed me into a cave in the canyon wall. It was a kind of waiting room where they left their supper guests while the village began the evening's celebrations. I hoped they might forget to post a guard, but they didn't. They left a big stone-faced ruffian to guard the entrance. I'd heard one of the coyotes call his name: Smash.

I paced around my cell for several minutes, hoping I might find a window, a crack, secret passageway, any weakness that might allow me to escape. No luck there, so I sat down and spent another several minutes studying the profile of my guard.

He had an unusual head, larger than the head of a normal coyote and not as pointed on the ears and nose. His body seemed heavier too, and his feet were huge, not the usual coyote paw that left a narrow track.

I thought about trying to strike up a conversation with him—I mean, what else did I have to do?—but he didn't look very friendly and, well, who wants to chat with a guy named Smash?

So I just sat there, listening to the hoots and shouts of the cannibals, and thinking that my luck had pretty muchly run out. Then, to my surprise,

I heard him say, "You know, buddy, what you did was really stupid."

I glanced around, thinking he might be speaking to someone else. I saw only the two of us. "Were you talking to me?"

He turned and glared at me. "I'm talking to you, yeah. Stupid behavior makes me angry." He stood up and paced toward me. "What did you expect to gain, quitting your ranch? One chicken dinner and then what?"

"Well, I . . ."

"Dumb, so dumb! You had a good job, a home, people who cared about you. You had it made, and you threw it all away."

"Look, I was all right until I heard their Chicken Chant and somehow . . . okay, it was the dumbest stunt I've ever pulled. I don't know how it happened."

He poked me in the chest with his paw. "I know how it happened. I know exactly how it happened, 'cause I did it, too."

"You?" I looked closer at his unusual head and body shape. "Wait! You're not a coyote, you're a dog!"

"That's right. I know your story 'cause it's my story."

"How'd you get here?"

He shrugged. "Stupid, like you. I had a great life, but was that enough? Naw. I wanted more. Fun, excitement, danger. I ran away from home and joined up with the coyotes, helped 'em raid chicken houses."

He began pacing a circle around me. "Oh, I was hot stuff! The coyotes didn't mess with me because, well, I had skills." He held up a huge paw and admired it, then brought it down like a hammer on a rock, breaking it into pieces. He grinned. "That's why they call me Smash." His smile faded. "It all started with one chicken dinner. It ruined my life. But the crazy thing is . . . I can't stand the taste of chicken anymore. It tastes like tuna fish."

"No kidding."

"Yeah. Ain't that a kick in the head?" He heaved a sigh. "What a waste. My poor mother cries herself to sleep every night, wondering where she went wrong. But it wasn't her fault. It was all me." His eyes stabbed me. "And look at *you*! Wouldn't your mother be ashamed if she could see you now?"

My head sank. "Yes, she would."

There was a moment of silence, then the silence was filled by the sounds of coyotes chanting in the distance. The words sent shivers down my spine.

Doggie, git the doggie, git the doggie
doggie!
Doggie, git the doggie, git the doggie
doggie!

Yum yum, eat 'em up, eat 'em up!
Yum yum, eat 'em up, eat 'em up!

Smash's eyes were boring holes in me. "You hear that?"

"I hear it, yes."

"They ain't kidding." He lumbered over to me. "What are you going to do, sit here like a rabbit and let 'em eat you?"

"I don't know what else to do."

He stuck his nose in my face and roared, "Break out, you bonehead! Run away, escape!"

"But you're guarding the door."

He gave that a moment's thought, then scowled and scratched the top of his head. "Good point. Never mind."

For several moments, neither of us spoke. Then I got an idea. "Wait! You can go with me. We'll bust out together."

"Me? Nah, it's too late for me."

"It's not too late. Think of your poor mother."

I knew right away that I'd said the wrong thing. His eyes turned wild and bloody, and he hissed,

"Don't you talk about my mother!" In a flash, he jumped on top of me and threw me to the floor. For a few terrible seconds, that hammer fist hung in the air, only inches away from my face. Then his eyes misted over, and he muttered, "Good old Mom. You reckon she'd be glad to see me again?"

"Of course she would."

"You don't think it's too late?"

"Smash, a mother never gives up hope."

He stepped away and gave me a look that almost froze my blood. I held my breath, wondering what he would say.

He said, "Let's boogie!"

I almost fainted with relief, but just then, Snort stepped up to the door of the cave and yelled, "Uh! Time for coyote supper, oh boy!"

I looked at Smash and he looked at me. What now?

The Coyotes Invade
the Ranch!

Smash's face gave no hint of what he would do next and I figured . . . well, that's it, I'm cooked. But then he walked over to Snort, gave him a friendly smile, and held up his fist. "See this?"

Snort looked closer at it. "Uh. Pretty big fits."

Smash nodded. "Now, watch this."

Wearing a silly grin, Snort watched as Smash began swinging his arm around in circles. On the third or fourth turn, he brought his hammer down on top of Snort's head. BAM! And fellers, the lights went out in Georgia. Old Snort dropped like a sack of cement, and he stayed down.

Smash acted as though it was no big deal. He stepped over the sleeping cannibal, glanced back at me and said, "Are you coming?"

I stared in amazement. "You made that look easy."

"Like I said, I have skills. Let's get out of here. They'll come after us."

We crept out of the cave and followed the canyon wall toward the south. Down below, the whole coyote village had turned out for the feast, and they were making a big celebration out of it. No doubt they would be disappointed when they learned that their supper had escaped.

Once we had gotten out of sight of the village, we pointed ourselves toward Ranch Headquarters and kicked up the speed. Behind us, the drumming stopped. There was a moment of silence, and then we heard the whoops and howls of angry cannibals. They had found my empty cell and seconds later, we heard them coming after us.

We kicked up the speed another notch, and I tossed a glance at Smash. He didn't appear to be worried. Good, because I was doing enough worrying for both of us. I mean, I'd had enough dealings with coyotes to know that you could cheat them every once in a while, but you sure didn't want to get caught doing it. They were not happy losers.

We flew across that big empty ranch country, up and down ravines, over sand draws, through sagebrush and cactus and catclaw brush, until at last I saw familiar sights looming up before us: the mailbox, the county road, and Ranch Headquarters. Seeing the house reminded me that I still had a job to do for Sally May.

"Smash, how do you feel about chicken dinners?"

"They taste like tuna fish."

"Okay, how do you feel about tuna fish?"

"Can't stand the stuff. Why?"

"Just checking. I have to save the chickens, and I didn't want to hire any guards who might get distracted."

He laughed. "Not me, brother. I've been to school on chickens." I felt his gaze lingering on me. "How about yourself?"

Slurp. "We're working on it."

He slowed to a walk and tapped the side of his head with a huge paw. "Look, it's all up here. Just think tuna fish."

"That's the problem. *I love tuna fish!*"

He roared with laughter. I didn't think it was so funny.

We entered the headquarters compound and I began searching for chickens. On an ordinary day, they would have been outside, pecking gravel and chasing bugs, but I didn't see a single bird. That meant they had holed up inside the chicken house, the very worst place they could have been.

I went thundering into the chicken house and, sure enough, there they sat on their roost, twenty-seven hens and one rooster, with their heads covered beneath their wings.

"Ranch Security! Coyote Alert! Everybody out, we're evacuating the building! Move, move, move!"

If I had set off a bomb, it would have had pretty much the same effect. I mean, in seconds we had birds flapping, squawking, screeching, bouncing off walls and the ceiling, flying in all directions . . . it was a circus.

J. T. Cluck flapped into a wall, hit the floor, and picked himself up. "It's about time you got here, dog. Did you hear the news? The British are coming!" He started running in circles, flapping his wings and screeching, "The British are coming! The British are coming!"

I grabbed him and gave him a shake. "J.T., the British aren't coming, but the coyotes *are*."

"Oh. Well, I knew it was someone. Who are the British, anyway?"

"Never mind. Get your hens out of here, head for the house, and roost in the trees."

He rubbed his chin and scowled. "You know, pooch, we don't much like trees."

I stuck my nose in his face and screamed, "*Get out of here, now!*"

"Well, you don't need to get all hateful about it."

He clapped his wings for attention and managed to get all his chickens back on the ground, and even quiet, and led them out the door. To my amazement, they walked in single file down to the house, and by the time the coyote army reached the northern perimeter of Ranch Headquarters, the birds were perched in trees beside the house.

Smash and I took up a forward position beside the yard gate and waited for the drama to begin. Just as I had figured, the coyotes went straight to the chicken house. I mean, those guys had done this before and knew the drill: you want money, you go to a bank; you want chickens, you go to a chicken house.

Heh heh. Boy, were they surprised. What they found inside was maybe a dozen feathers floating in the air and nary a chicken. They came out like a swarm of angry bees and saw me and Smash sitting beside the gate. For a moment of heartbeats, the situation looked pretty serious, a dozen inflamed cannibals facing two dogs.

But then . . . good old Smash. He made a hammer of his right fist and started swinging it

around and around. The coyotes stopped in their tracks, and all eyes turned to Scraunch.

Scraunch was furious. His eyes were flashing and he was grinding his teeth. He took two more steps toward us . . . and stopped. He opened his shark mouth and roared, "Mother of Hunk wear dirty socks!"

Whew! Right then, I knew we had won. When the enemy starts talking about your mother's dirty socks, it means he's out of ammo. So I gave it back to him. "Scraunch, your mother's so ugly, she couldn't get a date with a toad!"

"Ha! Mother of Hunk stink so bad, all flies drop dead, ho ho!"

"Oh yeah? Well, your mother . . ."

This went on, back and forth, for several minutes, and it might have stretched out into the night if Sally May hadn't come driving in from town. When the coyotes heard the car approaching, they began slinking away, then turned and vanished into the evening shadows.

Wow, what a finish! It turned out to be one of the most spectacular days of my whole career. When Sally May got out of her car, she stared in amazement at the scene before her—cannibals in flight, her entire flock of chickens decorating the trees, and the Head of Ranch Security standing tall at the yard gate.

Okay, I'd had a little help from Smash, and that surprised her too, a big unidentified, hammer-fisted dog sitting beside her yard gate. Slowly, she put the pieces together and rushed into the house.

A moment later, she came back outside with Loper and pointed up into the trees. "You didn't hear anything? What were you *doing*?"

Loper seemed amazed. "Well, Alfred and I were playing trucks."

Sally May rolled her eyes. "Honestly! Somebody could have jacked up the house and moved it to Amarillo!" Then she rushed out to the gate, where I was waiting.

It was delicious. I mean, she knelt down, threw her arms around my neck, and gave me such a fond embrace that I heard three vertebrae pop. As she hugged me, she whispered, "Hank, I don't care that you stink. You saved my chickens. You're a good dog!"

Standing nearby, Loper shrugged. "Well, if he's that good, maybe we'd better switch back to Co-op dog food. No more Cheapo, Hank."

Wow! What a finish! And it got even better. Guess who was watching from the iris patch. Guess who came scampering out the gate and tried to butt into my moment of glory. Guess who started rubbing against Sally May's ankles and got his tail stepped on.

Pete. I loved it!

And that's about the end of the . . . wait, there's one last detail: my old pal Smash. Loper and Sally May had no idea how he'd gotten to the ranch, and I wasn't able to explain it through tail wags, but it turned out okay. They kept him around the place for a week and ran a picture of him in the Twitchell paper. Sure enough, his people saw the ad and came out to the ranch to claim him.

I don't know where Smash is today, but I'll bet his momma's proud that he's not eating chickens. Neither am I, and fellers, this case is *slurp*.

Excuse me. This case is closed.

"Photogenic" Memory Quiz

We all know that Hank has a "photogenic" memory—being aware of your surroundings is an important quality for a Head of Ranch Security. Now you can test your powers of observation.

How good is your memory? Look at the illustration on page 4, and try to remember as many things about it as possible. Then, turn back to this page and see how many questions you can answer.

1. How many pockets were on Loper's shirt? 0, 1, or 2?

2. What was the name on the bag of dog food? Heap-O, Cut Rate-O, or Cheap-O?

3. Which hand did Loper have on the fencepost?

4. How many fenceposts were there? 2, 3, or 4?

5. What shape was Loper's belt buckle? Rectangular, oval, or square?

6. How many of Hank's paws could you see? 2, 3, 4, or all 6?

The following activities are samples from *The Hank Times,* the official newspaper of Hank's Security Force. Do not write on these pages unless this is your book. Even then, why not just find a scrap of paper?

For more games and activities like these, be sure to check out Hank's official website at **www.hankthecowdog.com**!

Eye-Crosserosis

I've done it again. I was staring at the end of my nose and had my eyes crossed for a long time. And you know what? They got hung up—my eyes, I mean. I couldn't get them uncrossed. It's a serious condition called Eye-Crosserosis. (You can read about the big problems Eye-Crosserosis caused me in my second book.) This condition throws everything out of focus, as you can see. Can you help me turn the double letters and word groupings below into words?

Insert the double letters into the word groupings to form words you can find in my books.

OO	NN	PP	CC	TT	LL
SS	ZZ	RR	FF	EE	OO

1. HAY_____

2. TTHPICK_____

3. KIY_____

4. AUAL_____

5. PULE_____

6. WD___WOOD___

7. COECT_____

8. SKIET_____

9. TTH_____

10. DEERT_____

11. AIDENT_____

12. BLUING_____

===

Answers:

1. HAPPY
2. TOOTHPICK
3. KITTY
4. ANNUAL
5. PUZZLE
6. WOOD
7. CORRECT
8. SKILLET
9. TEETH
10. DESSERT
11. ACCIDENT
12. BLUFFING

Hank Maze Craze

Pretend this maze has Hank
surrounded by coyotes! Help him
get out of the coyote village.

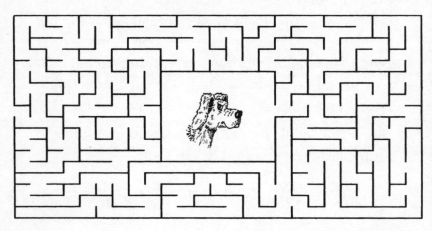

Answer on page 131

Rhyme Time

What would happen if Hank the Cowdog quit his job as Head of Ranch Security and began to look for other jobs? What jobs could he do?

When Hank runs into Rip and Snort, the coyote brothers, they call him Hunk. Make a rhyme using the name Hunk that would relate to the jobs described below.

Example: Hunk (Hank) could go to school and not study to do this: HUNK FLUNK

1. Hunk becomes a professional basketball player.

2. Hunk gets a vacant lot and fills it with old cars and iron scraps.

3. Hunk impersonates a black-and-white animal.

4. Hunk takes care of his nieces and nephews.

5. Hunk is a test subject for a machine that reduces things.

6. Hunk becomes a leaky boat.

7. Hunk goes to camp and gets a new bed.

8. Hunk retires to the Emerald Pond.

9. Hunk invents a new chocolate chip that is very, very thick.

10. Hunk becomes a car's luggage storage space.

Answers:

7. Hunk BUNK

1. Hunk DUNK	4. Hunk UNC	8. Hunk STUNK
2. Hunk JUNK	5. Hunk SHRUNK	9. Hunk CHUNK
3. Hunk SKUNK	6. Hunk SUNK	10. Hunk TRUNK

Have you read all of Hank's adventures?

Hank Maze Craze Answer

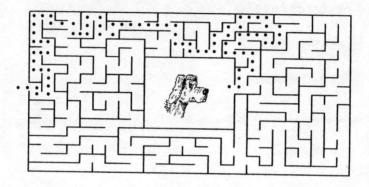

Join Hank the Cowdog's Security Force

Are you a big Hank the Cowdog fan? Then you'll want to join Hank's Security Force! Here is some of the neat stuff you will receive:

Welcome Package
- A Hank paperback
- An Original (19"x25") Hank Poster
- A Hank bookmark

Eight digital issues of
The Hank Times **with**
- Lots of great games and puzzles
- Stories about Hank and his friends
- Special previews of future books
- Fun contests

More Security Force Benefits
- Special discounts on Hank books, audios, and more
- Special Members Only section on website

Total value of the Welcome Package and *The Hank Times* is $23.99. However, your two-year membership is **only $7.99** plus $5.00 for shipping and handling.

☐ Yes I want to join Hank's Security Force. Enclosed is $12.99 ($7.99 + $5.00 for shipping and handling) for my **two-year membership**. [Make check payable to Maverick Books.]

Which book would you like to receive in your Welcome Package? (#____) any book except #50

_____

BOY or GIRL

YOUR NAME   (CIRCLE ONE)

_____

MAILING ADDRESS

_____

CITY   STATE   ZIP

_____

TELEPHONE   BIRTH DATE

_____

E-MAIL   (required for digital Hank Times)

Send check or money order for $12.99 to:
Hank's Security Force
Maverick Books
PO Box 549
Perryton, Texas 79070

DO NOT SEND CASH. NO CREDIT CARDS ACCEPTED.
Allow 2–3 weeks for delivery.
Offer is subject to change.

Photo Courtesy of Western Horseman Magazine

John R. Erickson, a former cowboy, has written numerous books for both children and adults and is best known for his acclaimed *Hank the Cowdog* series. He lives and works on his ranch in Perryton, Texas, with his family.

Gerald L. Holmes has illustrated numerous cartoons and textbooks in addition to the *Hank the Cowdog* series. He lives in Perryton, Texas.

Shawn Tevis Photography